WHY I'M ONLY
A JHEREG BARONET

I didn't notice where I was going, or how much time went by. I was swinging Spellbreaker as I walked, smacking it at buildings just to watch the walls crumble; or just flailing the chain wildly, hoping someone would get in my way.

Think about this. You've just made an enemy who can tail you wherever you go, and you've made him mad enough to kill you. So what do you do? Walk around without any protection making as big a spectacle of yourself as you can.

This is not what I call intelligent.

But *that* bright thought only came to me when I suddenly found myself surrounded by hostile faces. Several of them. I saw at least one wizard's staff. A voice came from somewhere inside of me. It sounded absurdly calm.

It said, "You're dead now, Vlad."

I felt the ground against my cheek . . .

> **"Steven Brust isn't afraid to stretch the boundaries of contemporary commercial fantasy."**
>
> **—NEWSDAY**

Ace Fantasy books by Steven Brust

STEVEN BRUST

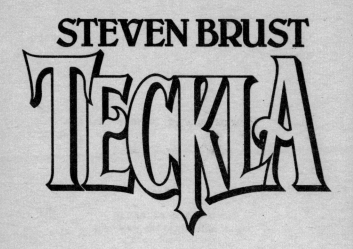

TECKLA

ACE FANTASY BOOKS
NEW YORK

My thanks to Adrian Morgan, for his invaluable assistance.

This book is an Ace Fantasy
original edition, and has never been
previously published.

TECKLA

An Ace Fantasy Book/published by arrangement with
the author and the author's agent, Valerie Smith

PRINTING HISTORY
Ace Fantasy edition/January 1987

ISBN: 0-441-79977-9

Ace Fantasy Books are published by The Berkley Publishing Group,
200 Madison Avenue, New York, New York 10016.
PRINTED IN THE UNITED STATES OF AMERICA

The Cycle

Phoenix sinks into decay
Haughty dragon yearns to slay.
Lyorn growls and lowers horn
Tiassa dreams and plots are born.
Hawk looks down from lofty flight
Dzur stalks and blends with night.
Issola strikes from courtly bow
Tsalmoth maintains though none knows
   how.
Vallista rends and then rebuilds
Jhereg feeds on others' kills.
Quiet torich won't forget
Shy chreotha weaves his net.
Yendi coils and strikes, unseen
Orca circles, hard and lean.
Frightened teckla hides in grass
Jhegaala shifts as moments pass
Athyra rules minds' interplay
Phoenix rise from ashes, gray.

This is the city: Adrilankha, Whitecrest.

The capital and largest city of the Dragaeran Empire contains all that makes up the domain, but in greater concentration. All of the petty squabbles within the seventeen Great Houses, and sometimes among them, become both more petty and more vicious here. Dragonlords fight for honor, Iorich nobles fight for justice, Jhereg nobles fight for money, and Dzurlords fight for fun.

If, in the course of this squabbling, a law is broken, the injured party may appeal to the Empire, which oversees the interplay of Houses with an impartiality that does credit to a Lyorn judging a duel. But the organization that exists at the core of House Jhereg operates illegally. The Empire is both unwilling and unable to enforce the laws and customs governing this inner society. Yet, sometimes, these unwritten laws are broken.

That's when I go to work. I'm an assassin.

Prologue

I found an oracle about three blocks down on Undauntra, a little out of my area. He wore the blue and white of the House of the Tiassa, and worked out of a hole-in-the-wall above a bakery, reached by climbing a long, knotted wooden stairway between crumbling walls to a rotting door. The inside of the place was about right. Leave it at that.

He wasn't busy, so I threw a couple of gold Imperials onto the table in front of him and sat opposite him on a shoddy octagonal stool that matched his. He looked to be a bit old, probably pushing fifteen hundred.

He glanced at the pair of jhereg riding my shoulders, but chose to pretend to be unexcited. "An Easterner," he said. Brilliant. "And a Jhereg." The man was a genius. "How may I serve you?"

"I have," I told him, "suddenly acquired more cash than I've ever dreamed of having. My wife wants me to build a castle. I could buy a higher title in the Jhereg—I'm now a baronet. Or I could use the money to expand my business. If I choose the latter, I risk, um, competition problems. How serious will these be? That's my question."

He put his right arm on the table and rested his chin on it, drumming the tabletop with the fingers of his left hand while staring up at me. He must have recognized me; how many Easterners are there who are high up in

2

the organization and wander around with jhereg on their shoulders?

When he'd looked at me long enough to be impressive, he said, "If you try to expand your business, a mighty organization will fall."

Well, la-dee-da. I leaned over the table and slapped him.

"*Rocza wants to eat him, boss. Can she?*"

"*Maybe later, Loiosh. Don't bother me.*"

To the Tiassa, I said, "I have a vision of you with two broken legs. I wonder if it's a true one?"

He mumbled something about sense of humor, and closed his eyes. After thirty seconds or so, I saw sweat on his forehead. Then he shook his head and brought out a deck of cards wrapped in blue velvet with his House insignia on them. I groaned. I hate Card readers.

"*Maybe he wants to play shereba,*" said Loiosh. I caught the faint psionic echo of Rocza laughing.

The oracle looked apologetic. "I wasn't getting anything," he explained.

"All right, all right," I said. "Let's get on with it."

After we went through the ritual, he tried to explain all the oracular meanings the Cards revealed to him. When I said, "Just the answers please," he looked hurt.

He studied the Mountain of Changes for a while, then said, "As far as I can see, m'lord, it doesn't matter. What's going to happen doesn't depend on any action you're going to take."

He gave me the apologetic look again. He must have practiced it. "That's the best I can do."

Splendid. "All right," I said. "Keep the change." That was supposed to be a joke, but I don't think he got it, so he probably still thinks I have no sense of humor.

I went back down the stairs and out onto Undauntra, a wide street packed full of craft shops on the east side and sparsely settled with small homes on the west, making it look oddly lopsided. About halfway back to my office, Loiosh said, "*Someone's coming, boss. Looks like muscle.*"

I brushed my hair back from my eyes with one hand and adjusted my cloak with the other, allowing me to check a few concealed goodies. I felt tension in Rocza's grip on my shoulder, but left it to Loiosh to calm her down. She was still new at this work.

"Only one, Loiosh?"

"Certain, boss."

"Okay."

About then, a medium-tall Dragaeran in the colors of House Jhereg (grey and black, if you're taking notes) fell into stride next to me. Medium-tall in a Dragaeran, you understand, made him a head and a half taller than I.

"Good afternoon, Lord Taltos," he said, pronouncing my name right.

I grunted back at him. His sword was light, worn at the hip, and clanked along between us. His cloak was full enough to conceal dozens of the same kind of things my cloak concealed sixty-three of.

He said, "A friend of mine would like to congratulate you on your recent successes."

"Thank him for me."

"He lives in a real nice neighborhood."

"I'm happy for him."

"Maybe you'd like to visit him sometime."

I said, "Maybe."

"Would you like to make plans for it?"

"Now?"

"Or later. Whatever's convenient for you."

"Where should we talk?"

"You name it."

I grunted again. In case that went too fast for you, this fellow had just informed me that he was working for an individual who was very high up in the Organization, and that said individual might want my services for something. In theory, it could be for any of a number of things, but there's only one thing that I'm known to do free-lance.

I took us a little further, until we were safely in my territory. Then I said, "All right," and steered us into an inn that jutted out a few feet onto Undauntra, and was one of the reasons merchants with hand-carts hated this part of the street.

We found an unoccupied end of a long table, and I sat down across from him without getting any splinters. Loiosh looked the place over for me and didn't say anything.

"I'm Bajinok," said my companion as the host brought us a bottle of fairly good wine and a couple of glasses.

"Okay."

"My friend wants some 'work' done around his house."

I nodded. Work, said that way, means wanting someone killed. "I know people," I said. "But they're all pretty busy right now." My last "work" had only been a few weeks before, and was, let's say, highly visible. I didn't feel like doing any more just then.

"Are you sure?" he asked. "This is just your style."

"I'm sure," I said. "But thank your friend for thinking of me. Another time, all right?"

"Okay," he said. "Another time."

He nodded to me, stood up, and left. And that should have been the end of it.

Verra, Demon-Goddess of my ancestors, may the water on thy tongue turn to ash. That should have been the end of it.

Farmday
Leffero, Nephews & Niece,
Launderers & Tailors
Malak Circle

fr: V. Taltos
Number 17, Garshos St.

Please do the following:

1 grey knit cotton shirt: remove wine stain from
rt sleeve, black tallow from lft & repair cut in rt
cuff.

1 pr grey trousers: remove blood stain from upper rt leg, klava stain from upper lft, & dirt
from knees.

1 pr black riding boots: remove reddish stain on
toe of rt boot, & remove dust & soot from both
& polish.

1 grey silk cravat: repair cut, & remove sweat
stains.

1 plain grey cloak: clean & press, remove cat
hairs, brush to remove white particles, remove
honing-oil stains, & repair cut in lft side.

1 Pocket Handkerchief: clean & press

Expect delivery by Homeday next.

> Yrs cordially,
> V. Taltos, Brnt, Jhrg (His seal)

1 –

**1 grey knit cotton shirt:
remove wine stain from rt sleeve. . .**

I stared out of the window onto streets I couldn't see and thought about castles. It was night and I was home, and while I didn't mind sitting in a flat looking at a street I couldn't see, I thought I might rather sit in a castle and look at a courtyard I couldn't see.

My wife, Cawti, sat next to me, her eyes closed, thinking about something or other. I sipped from a glass of a red wine that was too sweet. On top of a tall buffet was perched Loiosh, my jhereg familiar. Next to him was Rocza, his mate. Your basic conjugal scene.

I cleared my throat and said, "I visited an oracle last week."

She turned and stared at me. "You? Visiting an oracle? What's the world coming to? About what?"

I answered her last question. "About what would happen if I took all that money and plowed it into the business."

"Ah! That again. I suppose he told you something vague and mystical, like you'll be dead in a week if you try."

"Not exactly." I told her about the visit. Her face lost

its bantering look. I like her bantering look. But then, I like most of her looks.

"What do you make of it?" she said when I was finished.

"I don't know. You take that stuff more seriously than I do; what do you make of it?"

She chewed her lower lip for a while. Around then Loiosh and Rocza left the buffet and flew off down the hall, into a small alcove that was reserved for their privacy. It gave me ideas which I suppressed, because I dislike having my actions suggested to me by a flying reptile.

Finally, Cawti said, "I don't know, Vladimir. We'll have to wait and see, I guess."

"Yeah. Just something more to worry about. It's not as if we don't have enough—"

There was a thumping sound, as if someone were hitting the door with a blunt object. Cawti and I were up at almost the same instant, myself with a dagger, she with a pair of them. The wine glass I'd been holding dropped to the floor and I shook droplets off my hand. We looked at each other and waited. The thumping sound was repeated. Loiosh came tearing out of the alcove and came to rest on my shoulder, Rocza behind him, complaining loudly. I started to tell him to shut her up, but Loiosh must have because she became quiet. I knew this couldn't be a Jhereg attack, because the Organization doesn't bother you at home, but I had made more than one enemy outside of the Jhereg.

We moved toward the door. I stood on the side that would open, Cawti stood directly in front of it. I took a deep breath, let it out, and put my hand on the handle. Loiosh tensed. Cawti nodded. A voice from the other side said, "Hello? Is anyone there?"

I stopped.

Cawti's brows came together. She called out tentatively, "Gregory?"

The voice came back. "Yeah. Is that you, Cawti?"

She said, "Yes."

I said, "What the—?"

"It's all right," she said, but her voice lacked certainty and she didn't sheath her daggers.

I blinked a couple of times. Then it occurred to me that Gregory was an Eastern name. It was the Eastern custom to strike someone's door with your fist if you wanted to announce yourself. "Oh," I said. I relaxed a bit. I called out, "Come in."

A man, as human as I, started to enter, saw us, and stopped. He was small, middle-aged, about half bald, and startled. I suppose walking through a doorway to find three weapons pointing at you would be enough to startle anyone who wasn't used to it.

I smiled. "Come on in, Gregory," I said, still holding my dagger at his chest. "Drink?"

"Vladimir," said Cawti, I suppose hearing the edge in my voice. Gregory didn't move and didn't say anything.

"It's all right, Vladimir," Cawti told me directly.

"With whom?" I asked her, but I made my blade vanish and stood aside. Gregory stepped past me a bit gingerly, but not handling himself too badly, all things considered.

"I don't like him, boss," said Loiosh.

"Why not?"

"He's an Easterner; he ought to have a beard."

I didn't answer because I sort of agreed; facial hair is one of the things that sets us apart from Dragaerans, which was why I grew a mustache. I tried to grow a beard once, but Cawti threatened to shave it off with a rusty dagger after her second set of whisker burns.

Gregory was shown to a cushion, sitting down in a way that made me realize that he was prematurely balding rather than middle-aged. Cawti, weapons also gone, sat on the couch. I brought out some wine, did a little cooling spell, and poured us each a glass. Gregory nodded his thanks and sipped. I sat down next to Cawti.

"All right," I said. "Who are you?"

Cawti said, "Vlad. . . ." Then she sighed. "Vladimir,

this is Gregory. Gregory: my husband, the Baronet of Taltos.''

I saw perhaps the faintest of curl to his lip when she recited my title, and took an even stronger dislike to him. *I* can sneer at Jhereg titles; that doesn't mean anyone else can sneer at mine.

I said, ''Okay. We all know each other. Now, who are you, and what are you doing trying to knock down my door?''

His eyes flicked from Loiosh, perched on my right shoulder, to my face, to the cut of my clothes. I felt like I was being examined. This did nothing to improve my temper. I glanced over at Cawti. She bit her lip. She could tell I was becoming unhappy.

''Vladimir,'' she said.

''Hmmm?''

''Gregory is a friend of mine. I met him while visiting your grandfather a few weeks ago.''

''Go on.''

She shifted uncomfortably. ''There's a lot more to tell. I'd like to find out what he wants first, if I may.''

There was just the least bit of an edge to her voice, so I backed off.

''Should I take a walk?''

''Dunno. But thanks for asking. Kiss.''

I looked at him and waited. He said, ''Which question do you want me to answer first?''

''Why don't you have a beard?''

''What?''

Loiosh hissed a laugh. ''Never mind,'' I said. ''What do you want here?''

He looked back and forth between Cawti and me, then fixed his glance on her and said, ''Franz was killed yesterday evening.''

I glanced at my wife to see what effect this was having on her. Her eyes had widened slightly. I held my tongue.

After a pair of breaths, Cawti said, ''Tell me about it.''

Gregory had the nerve to glance significantly in my

direction. It almost got him hurt. He must have decided that I was all right, though, because he said, "He was standing at the door of the hall we'd rented, checking people, when someone just walked up to him and cut his throat. I heard the commotion and ran down, but whoever it was had vanished by the time I got there."

"Did anyone see him?"

"Not well. It was a Dragaeran though. They all—you —never mind. He was wearing black and grey."

"Sounds professional," I remarked, and Gregory looked at me in a way that you ought never to look at someone unless you are holding a blade at his throat. It was becoming difficult to let these things pass.

Cawti glanced at me quickly, then stood up. "All right, Gregory," she said. "I'll speak to you later."

He looked startled, and opened his mouth to say something, but Cawti gave him one of those looks she gives me when I carry a joke too far. She saw him to the door. I didn't stand up.

"All right," I said when she came back. "Tell me about it."

She studied me for a moment, as if looking at me for the first time. I knew enough not to say anything. Presently she said, "Let's take a walk."

There was no time in my life up to that point when I was as filled with so many strong, conflicting emotions as when we returned from that walk. No one, including Loiosh, had spoken during the last ten minutes, when I had run out of sarcastic questions and removed Cawti's need for terse, biting answers. Loiosh rhythmically squeezed alternate talons on my right shoulder, and I was subliminally aware of this and comforted by it. Rocza, who sometimes flies over our heads, sometimes rests on my other shoulder, and sometimes rests on Cawti's, was doing the last. The Adrilankhan air was cutting, and the endless lights of the city cast battling shadows before our feet as I found and opened the door to the flat.

We undressed and went to bed speaking only as

necessary and answering in monosyllables. I lay awake for a long time, moving as little as possible so Cawti wouldn't think I was lying awake. I don't know about her, but she didn't move much.

She arose before me the next morning and roasted, ground, and brewed the klava. I helped myself to a cup, drank it, and walked over to the office. Loiosh was with me; Rocza stayed behind. There was a cold, heavy fog in from the sea and almost no breeze—giving what is called "assassin's weather," which is nonsense. I said hello to Kragar and Melestav and sat down to brood and be miserable.

"Snap out of it, boss."

"Why?"

"Because you've got things to do."

"Like what?"

"Like finding out who shined the Easterner."

I thought that over for a moment. If you are going to have a familiar, it doesn't do to ignore him. "All right, why?"

He didn't say anything, but presently memories began to present themselves for my consideration. Cawti, as I'd seen her at Dzur Mountain after she had killed me (there's a story there, but never mind); Cawti holding me after someone else tried to kill me; Cawti holding a knife at Morrolan's throat and explaining how it was going to be, while I sat paralyzed and helpless; Cawti's face the first time I had made love with her. Strange memories, too—my emotions at the time, filtered through a reptilian mind that was linked to my own.

"Stop it, Loiosh!"

"You asked."

I sighed. "I suppose I did. But why did she have to get involved in something like that? Why—?"

"Why don't you ask her?"

"I did. She didn't answer."

"She would have if you hadn't been so—"

"I don't need advice on my marriage from a Verra-be-damned . . . no, I suppose I do, don't I? All right. What would you do?"

*"Ummm . . . I'd tell her that if I had two dead teckla
I'd give her one."*

"You're a lot of help."

"Melestav!" I yelled. "Send Kragar in here."

"Right away, boss."

Kragar is one of those people who are just naturally
unnoticeable. You could be sitting in a chair looking for
him and not realize that you were sitting in his lap. So I
concentrated hard on the door, and managed to see him
come in.

"What is it, Vlad?"

"Open your mind, my man. I have a face to give to
you."

"Okay."

He did, and I concentrated on Bajinok—the fellow
I'd spoken with a few days before, who had offered me
"work" that would be "just my style." Could he have
meant an Easterner? Yeah, maybe. He had no way of
knowing that to finalize an Easterner would defeat the
whole purpose of my having become an assassin in the
first place.

Or would it? Something nasty in my mind bade me
remember a certain conversation I'd recently had with
Aliera, but I chose not to think about it.

"Do you know him?" I asked Kragar. "Who does he
work for?"

"Yeah. He works for Herth."

"Ah ha."

"Ah ha?"

"Herth," I said, "runs the whole South Side."

"Where the Easterners live."

"Right. An Easterner was just killed. By one of us."

"Us?" said Loiosh. "Who is us?"

"A point. I'll think about it."

"What does that have to do with us?" asked Kragar,
introducing another meaning of us, just to confuse us.
Excuse me.

I said, "I don't know yet, but—Deathgate, I do
know. I'm not ready to talk about it yet. Could you set
me up a meeting with Herth?"

He tapped his fingers on the arm of his chair and looked at me quizzically. It wasn't usual for me to leave him in the dark about things like that, but he finally said, "Okay," and left.

I took out a dagger and started flipping it. After a moment I said to Loiosh, *"She still could have told me about it."*

"She tried. You weren't interested in discussing it."

"She could have tried harder."

"It wouldn't have come up if this hadn't happened. And it is her own life. If she wants to spend half of it in the Easterners' ghetto, rabble-rousing, that's her—"

"It hardly sounds like rabble-rousing to me."

"Ah," said Loiosh.

Which shows how much good it is to try to get the better of your familiar.

I'd rather skip over the next couple of days, but as I had to live them, you can at least put up with a sketch. For two solid days Cawti and I hardly exchanged a word. I was mad that she hadn't told me about this group of Easterners, and she was mad because I was mad. Once or twice I'd say something like, "If you'd—", then bite it back. I'd notice that she was looking at me hopefully, but I'd only notice too late, and then I'd stalk out of the room. Once or twice she'd say something like, "Don't you even care—", and then stop. Loiosh, bless his heart, didn't say anything. There are some things that even a familiar can't help you work out.

But it's a hell of a thing to go through days like that. It leaves scars.

Herth agreed to meet me at a place I own called The Terrace. He was a quiet little Dragaeran, only half a head taller than I, with an almost bashful way of dropping his eyes. He came in with two enforcers. I also had two, a fellow who was called Sticks because he liked to beat people with them, and one named Glowbug, whose eyes would light up at the oddest times. The enforcers found good positions for doing what they were paid for.

Herth took my suggestion and ordered the pepper-sausage, which is better tasted than described.

As we were finishing up our Eastern-style desert pancakes (which, really, no one should make except Valabar's, but these were all right), Herth said, "So what can I do for you?"

I said, "I have a problem."

He nodded, dropping his eyes again as if to say, "Oh, how could little me help someone like you?"

I went on, "There was an Easterner finalized a few days ago, by a professional. It happened in your area, so I was wondering if, maybe, you could tell me a bit about what happened, and why."

Now, there were several possible answers he could have given me. He could have explained as much as he knew about it, he could have smiled and claimed ignorance, he could have asked me what my interest was. Instead, he looked at me, stood up, and said, "Thanks for the dinner; I'll see you again, maybe." Then he left.

I sat there for a while, finishing my klava. *"What do you make of that, Loiosh?"*

"I don't know, boss. It's funny that he didn't ask why you wanted to find out. And if he knows, why did he agree to the meeting in the first place?"

"Right," I said.

I signed the bill and left, Sticks and Glowbug preceding me out of the place. When we reached the office I told them to take off. It was evening, and I was usually done by that time, but I didn't feel like going back home just then. I changed weapons, just to kill time. Changing weapons is something I do every two or three days so that no weapon is around my person enough to pick up my aura. Dragaeran sorcery can't identify auras, but Eastern witchcraft can, and should the Empire ever decide to employ a witch—

"I'm an idiot, Loiosh."

"Yeah, boss. Me, too."

I finished changing weapons and made it home quickly.

"Cawti!" I yelled.

She was in the dining room, scratching Rocza's chin. Rocza leapt up and began flying around the room with Loiosh, probably telling him about her day. Cawti stood up, looking at me quizzically. She was wearing trousers of Jhereg grey that fit low on her hips, and a grey jerkin with black embroidery. She glanced at me with an expression of remote inquiry, her head tilted to the side, her brows raised in that perfect face, surrounded by sorcery-black hair. I felt my pulse quicken in a way that I had been afraid it wouldn't any more.

"Yes?" she said.

"I love you."

She closed her eyes then opened them again, not saying anything. I said, "Do you have the weapon?"

"Weapon?"

"The Easterner who was killed. Was the weapon left there?"

"Why, yes, I suppose someone has it."

"Get it."

"Why?"

"I doubt whoever it was knows about witchcraft. I'll bet I can pick up an aura."

Her eyes grew wide, then she nodded. "I'll get it," she said, and reached for her cloak.

"Shall I go with you?"

"No, I don't. . . ." Then, "Sure, why not?"

Loiosh landed on my shoulder and Rocza landed on Cawti's and we went down the stairs into the Adrilankha night. In some ways things were better, but she didn't take my arm.

Is this starting to depress you? Heh. Good. It depressed me. It's much easier to deal with someone you only have to kill. As we left my area and began to cross over into some of the rougher neighborhoods, I hoped someone would jump me so I could work out some of what I was feeling.

Our feet went *clack clack* to slightly differing rhythms, occasionally synchronizing, then falling apart. Sometimes I'd try to change my step to keep them together, but it didn't do much. Our paces were our usual compromise, worked out long ago, between the shorter steps she was most comfortable with and my longer ones. We didn't speak.

You identify the Eastern section first by its smell. During the day the whole neighborhood is lousy with open-air cafes, and the cooking smells are different from anything the Dragaerans have. In the very early morning the bakeries begin to work; the aroma of fresh Eastern bread reaches out like tendrils to gradually take over the night smells. But the night smells, when the cafes are closed and the bakeries haven't started, are the smells of rotting food and human and animal waste. At night the wind blows across the area, toward the sea, and the prevailing winds are from the slaughterhouses northwest of town. It's as if only at night can the area's true colors, to mix a metaphor, come to the surface.

The buildings are almost invisible at night. Lamps or candles glowing in a few windows provide the only light, so the nature of the structures around you is hidden, yet the streets are so narrow that sometimes there is hardly room to walk between the buildings. There are places where doors in buildings opposite each other cannot be opened at the same time. At times you feel as if you were walking through a cave or in a jungle, and your boots tramp through garbage more often than on the hard-packed rutted dirt of the street.

It's funny to go back there. On the one hand, I hate it. It is everything that I've worked to get away from. But on the other, surrounded by Easterners, I feel a tension drain out of me that I don't notice except when it is gone; and it hits me again that, to a Dragaeran, I am an *other*.

We reached the Eastern section of town past midnight. The only people awake at that hour were derelicts and those who preyed on derelicts. Both groups avoided us, according us the respect given to anyone who walks as if he was above any dangers in a dangerous area. I would be lying if I said that I wasn't pleased to notice this.

We reached a place where Cawti knew to enter. The

"door" was a doorway covered by a curtain. I couldn't see a thing inside, but I had the feeling I was in a narrow hallway. The place stank. Cawti called out, "Hello."

There were faint rustling sounds, then, "Is someone there?"

"It's Cawti."

Heavy breathing, rustling, a few other voices mumbling, then flint was struck, there was a flash of light, and a candle was lit. It hurt my eyes for a moment. We were standing in front of a doorway without even a curtain. The inside of the room held a few bodies that were stirring. To my surprise, the room was, as far as I could tell in the light of single candle, clean and uncluttered except for the blanketed forms. There was a table and a few chairs. A pair of beady eyes was staring at us from a round face behind the candle. The face belonged to a short, very fat male Easterner in a pale dressing gown. The eyes rested on me, flicked to Loiosh, Cawti, Rocza, and came back to me.

"Come in," he said. "Sit down." We did, as he went around the room to light a few more candles. As I sat in a soft, cushioned chair, I counted a total of four persons on the floor. As they sat up, I saw that one was a slightly plump woman with greying hair, another was a younger woman, the third was my old friend Gregory, and the fourth was a male Dragaeran, which startled me. I studied his features until I could place his House, and when I identified him as a Teckla I didn't know whether to be less surprised or more.

Cawti seated herself next to me. She nodded to all present and said, "This is my husband, Vladimir." Then she indicated the fat man who had been up first and said, "This is Kelly." We exchanged nods. The older woman was called Natalia, the younger one was Sheryl, and the Teckla was Paresh. She didn't supply patronymics for the humans and I didn't push it. We all mumbled hellos.

Cawti said, "Kelly, do you have the knife that was found by Franz?"

Kelly nodded. Gregory said, "Wait a minute. I never

mentioned a knife being left by his body."

I said, "You didn't have to. You said it was a Jhereg who did it."

He grimaced at me, screwing his face up.

"Can I eat him, boss?"

"Shut up, Loiosh. Maybe later."

Kelly looked at me, which means he fixed me with his squinty eyes and tried to see through me. That's what it felt like, anyway. He turned to Cawti and said, "Why do you want it?"

"Vladimir thinks we might be able to find the assassin from the blade."

"And then?" said Kelly, turning to me.

I shrugged. "Then we find out who he worked for."

Natalia, from the other side of the room, said, "Does it matter for whom he worked?"

I just shrugged. "It doesn't matter to me. I thought it might to you."

Kelly went back to staring at me through his little pig eyes; I was amazed to discover that he was actually making me uncomfortable. He nodded a little, as if to himself, then left the room for a moment, returning with a knife wrapped in a piece of cloth that had probably once been part of a sheet. He handed cloth and weapon to Cawti. I nodded and said, "We'll be in touch."

We walked out the door. The Teckla, Paresh, had been standing in front of it. He moved aside as we headed toward the door, but not as quickly as I would have expected. Somehow that struck me as significant.

It was still several hours until sunrise as we made our way back toward our part of town. I said, "So, these are the people who are going to take over the Empire, huh?"

Cawti gestured with the bundle she held in her left hand. "Someone thinks so," she said.

I blinked. "Yeah. I guess someone does."

The stench of the Eastern area seemed to linger much further on the way back to our flat.

2⁼

. . .black tallow from left. . .

Down in the basement under my office is a little room that I call "the lab," an Eastern term that I picked up from my grandfather. The floor is hard-packed dirt, the walls are bare, mortared rock. There is a small table in the center and a chest in the corner. The table holds a brazier and a couple of candles. The chest holds all sorts of things.

Early in the afternoon of the day after we procured the knife, the four of us—Cawti, Loiosh, Rocza and me—trooped down to this room. I unlocked it and led the way in. The air was stale and smelled faintly of some of the things in the chest.

Loiosh sat on my left shoulder. He said, *"Are you sure you want to do this, boss?"*

I said, *"What's that supposed to mean?"*

"Are you sure you're in the right frame of mind to cast spells?"

I thought about that. A caution from one's familiar is something that no witch in his right mind dismisses without consideration. I glanced at Cawti, who was waiting patiently, and maybe guessing some of what I was thinking about. There was a lot of emotional mayhem hammering around my insides. This can be

21

good, as long as it can be put into the spell. But I was also in something of a funk, and when I get that way I mostly feel like sleeping. If I didn't have energy to direct the spell, it could get out of control.

"It'll be all right," I told him.

"Okay, boss."

I dumped the old ashes out of the brazier into a corner of the room and made a mental note to myself to clean that corner one of these days. I opened the chest and Cawti helped me put new coals into the brazier. I tossed away the old black candles and replaced them. Cawti positioned herself to my left, holding the knife. I called upon my link to the Orb and caused the wick of one of the candles to become hot enough to ignite. I used it to light the other candle, and, with some work, the coals in the brazier. I put this and that into the fire and set the dagger in question before it.

It's all symbolic, you know.

I mean, I sometimes wonder if it would work with water that I only *thought* had been purified (whatever "purified" means). And what if I used incense that smelled right, but was just ordinary incense? What if I used thyme that someone just picked up at the market on the corner, and told me was off a ship from the East? I don't know, and I don't think I'll ever find out, but I suspect it wouldn't matter. Every once in a while, you find something that really *is* all in the mind.

But these thoughts form the before and after of the spell. The during is all sensation. Rhythms pulse through you in time to the flickering of candles. You take yourself and plunge or are plunged into the heart of the flames until you are *elsewhere*, and you blend with the coals and Cawti is there beside you and inside you weaving in and out of the bonds of shadow you build that ensnare you like a small insect in a blue earth derivative and you find you have touched the knife and now you *know* it for a murder weapon, and you begin to feel the person who held it, and your hand goes through the delicate slicing motion he used and you drop it, as he did, his work done, as is yours.

I pushed it a little, trying to glean all I could from the moment of the casting. His name occurred to me, as something I'd known all along which chose to creep into my consciousness just at this moment, and about then that part of me that was really Loiosh became aware that we were on the down side of the enchantment and began to relax the threads that guarded the part of Loiosh that was me.

It was about there that I realized something was wrong. There is a thing that happens when witches work together. You don't know the other witch's thought; it is more that you are thinking his thoughts for him. And so, for a moment, I was thinking about me, and I became aware that there was a core of bitterness in me, directed at me, and it shook me.

There was never the danger Loiosh had feared, largely because he was there. The spell was drifting apart by then anyway, and we were all carefully letting go and drifting with it, but a big lump formed itself in my throat, and I twitched, knocking over a candle. Cawti reached forward to steady me and we locked eyes for a moment as the last of the spell flickered and collapsed and our minds became our own again.

She dropped her eyes, knowing that we had felt what we had felt.

I opened the door to let the smoke out into the rest of the building. I was a bit tired, but it hadn't been all that difficult a spell. Cawti and I went back up the stairway next to each other but not touching. We were going to have to talk, but I didn't know what to say. No, that wasn't it; I just couldn't make myself.

We went into my office and I yelled for Kragar. Cawti sat in his chair. Then she yelped and stood up upon discovering that he was in it. I smiled a bit at Kragar's innocent look. It was probably funnier than that, but we were feeling the tension.

I said, "His name is Yerekim. I've never heard of him. Have you?"

Kragar nodded. "He's an enforcer for Herth."

"Exclusively?"

"I think so. I'm pretty certain. Should I check?"

"Yes."

He simply nodded, rather than making a comment about being overworked. I think Kragar picks up on more than he admits. After he had slithered out of the room, Cawti and I sat in silence for a moment. Then she said, "I love you, too."

Cawti went home, and I spent part of the day getting in the way of people who worked for me and trying to act as if I ran my business. The third time Melestav, my secretary, mentioned what a nice day it was I took the hint as well as the rest of the day off.

I wandered through the streets, feeling powerful, as a force behind so much of what happened in the area, and insignificant, because it mattered so little. But I did get my thoughts in order, and made some decisions about what I would do. Loiosh asked me if I knew why I was doing it and I admitted that I didn't.

The breeze came from the north for a change, instead of in from the sea. Sometimes the north wind can be brisk and refreshing. I don't know, maybe it was my state of mind, but then it just felt chilly.

It was a lousy day. I resolved not to listen to Melestav's opinion on the weather anymore.

By the next morning Kragar had confirmed that, yes, Yerekim worked only for Herth. Okay. So Herth wanted this Easterner dead. That meant that it was either something personal about this Easterner—and I couldn't conceive of a Jhereg having a personal grudge against an Easterner—or this group was, in some way, a threat or an annoyance.

That was most likely, and certainly a puzzle.

"Ideas, Loiosh?"

"Just questions, boss. Like, who would you say is leader of that group?"

"Kelly. Why?"

"The Easterner they shined—Franz—why him instead of Kelly?"

In the next room, Melestav was riffling through a stack of papers. Above me, someone was tapping his foot. Sounds of a muted conversation came through the fireplace from somewhere unknown. The building was still, yet seemed to breathe.

"Right," I said.

It was around the middle of the afternoon when Loiosh and I found ourselves back in the Easterners' quarter. I couldn't have found the place no matter how hard I looked, but Loiosh was able to pick it out at once. In the daylight, it was another low, squat, brown building, with a pair of tiny windows flanking the door. Both windows were covered by boards, which went a long way toward explaining how stuffy it had been.

I stood outside the curtained doorway, started to clap, stopped, and banged on the wall. After a moment the Teckla, Paresh, appeared. He positioned himself in the middle of the doorway, as if to block it, and said, "Yes?"

"I'd like to see Kelly."

"He is not here." His voice was low, and he spoke slowly, pausing before each sentence as if he were organizing it in his head before committing it to the air. He had the rustic accent of the duchies to the immediate north of Adrilankha, but his phrasings were more those of a Chreotha or Vallista craftsman, or perhaps a Jhegaala merchant. Odd.

"Do you believe him, Loiosh?"

"I'm not sure."

So I said, "Are you quite certain?"

Something flickered then—a twitching at the corners of his eyes—but he only said, "Yes."

"There's something weird about this guy, boss."

"I noticed."

"There's something weird about you," I told him.

"Why? Because I'm not trembling in fear at the mere sight of your colors?"

"Yeah."

"I'm sorry to disappoint you."

"Oh, I'm not disappointed," I said. "Intrigued, maybe."

He studied me for a moment, then stepped back from the doorway. "Come in, if you want," he said.

I didn't have anything better to do just then, so I followed him in. The room didn't smell much better during the day, with its windows boarded shut. It was lit by two small oil lamps. He indicated a cushion on the floor. I sat down. He brought in an Eastern wine that was mostly water and slopped some into chipped porcelain cups, then sat facing me. He said, "I intrigue you, you say. Because I don't seem to fear you."

"You have an unusual disposition."

"For a Teckla."

I nodded.

We sipped our wine for a while, the Teckla looking off into space while I studied him. Then he started talking. I listened to what he said, becoming more and more intrigued as he spoke. I don't know that I understand all of it, but I'll give it to you as I remember it and you can decide for yourself.

You're titled, aren't you? Baron, isn't it? Baronet, then. All right. It doesn't really matter to you, I know. We both know what Jhereg titles are worth; I daresay you know to the nearest copper penny. The Orca *do* care; they make certain that orders of nobility are given or withdrawn whenever it's proper, so the quartermaster is of a higher rank than the bosun, yet lower than the mate. You didn't know that, did you? But I've heard of a case where an Orca was stripped of her county, granted a barony, stripped of that, given a duchy, then another county, then stripped of both and given her original county back, all within the same forenoon. A bookkeeping error, I was told.

But, do you know, none of those counties or duchies really existed. There are other Houses like that, too.

In the House of the Chreotha, titles are strictly hereditary, and lifelong unless something unusual happens, but there, too, they are not associated with any land.

But you have a baronetcy, and it is real. Have you ever been there? I can see by the look on your face that it never occurred to you to visit it. How many families live in your dominion, Baronet Taltos? That's all? Four? Yet it has never occurred to you to visit them.

I'm not surprised. Jhereg think that way. Your domain is within some nameless barony, possibly empty, and that within a county, maybe also empty, and that within a duchy. Of what House is your Duke, Baronet? Is he a Jhereg, also? You don't know? That doesn't surprise me, either.

What am I getting at? Just this: Of all the "Noble Houses"—which means every House except my own—there are only a few which contain any of the aristocracy, and then only a few of that House. Most of those in the House of the Lyorn are Knights, because only the Lyorns continue to treat titles as they were when first created, and Knight is a title that has no land associated with it. Have you thought of that, most noble Jhereg? These titles were associated with holdings. Military holdings, at first, which is why most of the domains around here are those of Dragonlords; this was once the Eastern edge of the Empire, and Dragons have always been the best military leaders.

My master was a Dzurlord. Her great-grandfather had earned the title of Baron during the Elde Island wars. My master had distinguished herself before the Interregnum during some war with the East. She was old, but still healthy enough to go charging off to do one thing or another. She was rarely at home, yet she was not unkind. She did not forbid her Teckla to read, as many do, and I was fortunate enough to be taught at an early age, though there was little enough reading matter to be found.

I had an older sister and two younger brothers. Our fee, for our thirty acres, was one hundred bushels of wheat or sixty bushels of corn, our choice. It was steep, but rarely above our means, and our master was understanding during lean years. Our closest neighbor to the west paid one hundred and fifty bushels of wheat for twenty-eight acres, so we counted ourselves lucky and helped him when he needed it. Our neighbor to the north had thirty-five acres, and he owed two gold Imperials, but we saw little of him so I don't know how hard or easy his lot was.

When I reached my sixtieth year I was granted twenty acres a few miles south of where my family lived. All of the neighbors came and helped me clear the land and put up my home, which I made large enough for the family I hoped to have someday. In exchange, I had to send to my master four young kethna every year, so by necessity I raised corn to feed them.

After twenty years I had paid back, in kind, the loans of kethna and seedlings that had gotten me started, and I thought myself well off—especially as I'd gotten used to the stench of a kethna farm. More, there was a woman I'd met in Blackwater who still lived at home, and there was, I think, something between us.

It was on an evening late in the spring of my twenty-first year on my own that I heard sounds far to the south. Cracking sounds, as a tree will make when it begins to topple, but far, far louder. That night, I saw red flames to the south. I stood outside of my house to watch, and I wondered.

After an hour, the flames filled the sky, and the sounds were louder. Then came the greatest yet. I was, for a moment, blinded by a sudden glare. When the spots cleared from my eyes I saw what seemed to be a sheet of red and yellow fire hanging over my head, as if it were about to descend on me. I think I screamed in terror and ran for my house. By the time I was inside the sheet had descended, and all of my lands were burning, and my house as well, and that was when I looked fully upon death. It seemed to me then, Lord Taltos, that I had not had enough of a life for it to end that way. I called upon Barlan, he of the Green Scales, but he had, I guess, other calls to make. I called upon Trout, but he brought me no water to dampen the flames. I even asked Kelchor, Goddess of the cat-centaurs, to carry me from that place, and my answer was smoke that choked me and sparks that singed my hair and eyebrows and a creaking, splintering groan as part of the house fell in.

Then I thought of my springhouse. I made it out the door and somehow lived through the flames that, my memory tells me, reached taller than I, and made it there. It was built of stone, of course, for the dampness would have rotted timber, so it still stood. I was badly burned, but I made it into the stream.

I lay there trembling for what must have been the whole night and into the day. The water was warm, even hot, but still cooler than the air around it. I fell asleep in that stream, and when I awoke—well, I will not try to describe the desolation around me. It was only then, I am ashamed to say, that I thought of my livestock, who had died during the night as I nearly had. But there was nothing to be done for them now.

And what did I do then, Baronet? Laugh if you will, but my first thought was that I could not pay my master for the year, and must go throw myself on her mercy. Surely, I thought, she would understand. So I began to walk toward her keep—southward.

Ah! I see that you have thought it out. So did I, as I began to take my first steps. Southward was where her castle stood, and southward was the origin of the flames. I stopped and considered for some time, but eventually I continued, for I had nowhere else to go.

It was many miles, and all I saw around me as I walked were burnt-out homes and charred ground, and blackened woods that had never been cleared, until now. Not another soul did I see during the entire journey. I came to the place where I had been born and had lived most of my life, and I saw what was left.

I performed the rites as best I could for them, and I think I was too numb to realize what it meant. When I had finished I continued my journey, sleeping in an empty field, warmed by the ground itself, which still felt the heat from the scorching it had endured.

I came to the keep and, to my surprise, it seemed unharmed. Yet the gate was closed, and no one answered my calls. I waited outside for minutes, hours, finally the whole day and that night. I was ravenously hungry and called out from time to time, but no one answered.

At last it was, I think, hunger more than anything else that led me to climb over the walls. It wasn't difficult, since none opposed me. I found a burnt log that was long enough, dragged it to the wall, and used it as a ladder.

There was no living being in the courtyard. I saw half a dozen bodies dressed in Dzur livery. I stood there and trembled, cursing my stupidity for not having brought food from the springhouse.

I think I stood there for an hour before I dared to enter, but eventually I did. I found the larder and ate. Slowly, over the course of weeks, I gathered the courage to search the keep. During this time I slept in the stables, not daring to make use of even the servant's quarters. I found a few more bodies in my search, and burned them as best I could, though, as I said, I knew few of the rites. Most of them were Teckla—some I recognized, a few I had once called friends—gone to serve the master, and now gone forever. What became of my master I never found out, for I think none of the bodies was hers.

I ruled that castle then, Baronet. I fed the livestock with the grain that had been hoarded there, and butchered them as I needed. I slept in the lord's bedchamber, ate her food, and, most of all, I read her books. She had tomes on sorcery, Baronet. A library full of them. And history, and geography, and stories. I learned much. I practiced sorcery, which opened before me a whole world, and the spells I'd known before seemed only games.

Most of a year passed in this way. It was late in the winter when I heard the sounds of someone pulling on the bell rope. The old fear that is my heritage as a Teckla, and at which you, my Lord Jhereg, must take such delight in sneering, came back then. I trembled and looked for a place to hide.

But then something came over me. Perhaps it was the magic I had learned; perhaps it was that all I had read had made me feel insignificant, and fear therefore seemed foolish; perhaps it was simply that, having survived the fire, I had learned the full measure of terror. But I didn't hide. Instead I went down the great winding stairway of what I now thought of as my home and threw open the doors.

Before me stood a noble of the House of the Lyorn. He was very tall and about my age, and wore a golden-brown, ankle-length skirt, a bright red shirt and a short fur cape. He wore a sword at his belt and a pair of vambraces. He didn't wait for me to speak, simply saying, "Inform your master that the Duke of Arylle will see him."

What I felt then is, I suppose, something you have felt often, but I never had before. That amazing, delicious rush of anger that a boar must feel when it charges the hunter, not really aware that it is overmatched in every way except ferocity, and is why the boar sometimes wins, and the hunter is always afraid. But there he stood, in *my* castle, and asked to see my master.

I stepped back a pace, drew myself up, and said, "I am master here."

He barely glanced at me. "Don't be absurd," he said. "Fetch your master at once or I'll have you beaten."

I had read quite a bit by then, and what I had read put the words into mouth that my heart wanted to speak. "My Lord," I said, "I have told you that I am master here. You are in my home, and you are lacking in courtesy. I must ask you to leave."

Then he did look at me, with such contempt that, had I been in any other frame of mind, it alone would have crushed me. He reached for his sword, I think now only to beat me with the flat, but he never drew it. I called upon my new skills and threw a blast at him that, I thought, would have burnt him down on the spot.

He gestured with his hands, and looked startled, but he seemed to take me seriously for the first time. That, my good Baronet, was a victory that I shall always treasure. The look of respect that came over him was as delicious to me as a cool drink to a man dying of thirst.

He hurled a spell at me. I knew I could not stop it, but I ducked out of the way. It exploded against the far wall behind me in a mass of flame and smoke. I threw something at him, then ran back up the stairs.

For the next hour I led him on a merry chase throughout the keep, stinging him with my spells and hiding before he could destroy me with his. I think that I laughed and mocked him, too, although I cannot say for certain.

At length, though, as I stopped to rest, I realized that he would surely kill me eventually. I managed to teleport myself back to the springhouse I knew so well.

I never saw him again. Perhaps he had come to ask about tribute he was due, I don't know. But I was changed. I made my way to Adrilankha using my new sorcerous skills for money among the Teckla households I passed. A skilled sorcerer willing to work for the pittance a Teckla can pay is rare, so, with time, I accumulated a goodly sum. When I came to the city, I found a poor, drunken Issola who was willing to teach Court manners and speech for what I could afford to pay. No doubt he taught me poorly by Court standards, yet I learned enough so that I could work with my equals in the city and compete fairly, I thought, as a sorcerer.

I was wrong, of course. I was still a Teckla. A Teckla who fancied himself a sorcerer was, perhaps, amusing, but those who need spells to prevent burglary, or to cure addictions, or secure the foundations of buildings, will not take a Teckla seriously.

I was destitute when I found my way to the Easterners' quarter. I will not pretend that life has been easy here, for Easterners have no more love for humans than most humans do for Easterners, yet my skills were, at least sometimes, useful.

As for the rest, Lord Taltos, suffice it to say that I chanced to meet Franz, and I spoke of life as a Teckla, and he spoke of the common thread that connects the Teckla and the Easterner, and of bare survival for our peoples, and of hope that it needn't always be this way.

He introduced me to Kelly, who taught me to see the world around me as something I could change—something I *had* to change.

Then I began to work with Franz. Together we found more Teckla, both here and those who slaved under masters far more vicious than my own. And when I would speak of the terror of the Empire under which we all suffered, Franz would speak of hope that, together, we could make a world free from terror. Hope was always half of his message, Baronet Taltos. And action was the other half—building hope through our own actions. And if, from time to time, we didn't know how, Kelly would lead us to discover it ourselves.

They were a team, my good Jhereg. Kelly and Franz. When someone fails at a task, Kelly can verbally tear him to pieces; but Franz was always there to help him try again, in the streets. Nothing frightened him. Threats pleased him, because they showed he was scaring someone, and proved we were on a good path. That was Franz, Lord Taltos. That was why they killed him.

I hadn't asked why they had killed him.

But all right. I chewed over his story for a few minutes. "Paresh," I said, "what was that about threats?"

He stared at me for a moment, as if I'd just seen a mountain collapse and asked of what kind of stone it was made. Then he turned his face away. I sighed. "All right," I said. "When will Kelly be back?"

He faced me again, and his expression was like a closed door. "Why do you want to know?"

Loiosh squeezed my shoulder with his talons. *"Take it easy,"* I told him. To Paresh I said, "I want to speak with him."

"Try tomorrow."

I thought about trying to explain myself to him so he would, perhaps, answer me. But he was a Teckla. Whatever else he was, he was still a Teckla.

I stood up and let myself out and walked back to my side of town.

3 -

& repair cut in rt cuff

When I arrived on familiar ground again it was early
evening. I saw no reason to return to the office so I
made my way toward home.

One was lounging against a wall on Garshos, near
Copper Lane. Loiosh started to warn me just about the
time I noticed the guy, which was just as he noticed me.
Then Loiosh said, *"There's another one behind you."*

I said, *"Okay."* I wasn't too worried, because if
they'd wanted to kill me I would never have seen them.
When I reached the one in front of me he was blocking
my path, and I recognized him as Bajinok, which meant
Herth—the guy who ran South Adrilankha. My shoulders went limp and my hands twitched. I stopped a few
paces away from him. Loiosh watched the one behind
me. Bajinok looked down at me and said, "I've got a
message."

I nodded, guessing at what it was.

He continued, "Stay away. Keep out of it."

I nodded again.

He said, "Do you agree?"

I said, "Can't do it, I'm afraid."

His hand went to his sword hilt, just as an idle,
threatening gesture. He said, "Are you sure?"

"I'm sure."

"I could make the message more explicit," he said.

Since I didn't feel like having my leg broken just then I threw a knife at him, underhanded. This was something I'd spent a lot of time practicing, because it is so fast. I don't know of anyone who has ever been seriously injured by a knife thrown that way except by me, and even with me it takes a lot of luck. On the other hand, *anyone* will flinch.

While he was busy flinching, and the knife was hitting him hilt first in the stomach, Loiosh was flying into the face of the other one. I had my rapier out before Bajinok had recovered, and I used the time to step out into the street to make sure neither of them could get behind me.

Bajinok's sword was in his hand by then and he had a dagger in the other. He was just coming into a guard position when my point took him in the right leg, above the knee. He cursed and stepped back. I followed and put a cut across the left side of his face, and, with the same motion, a good, deep one on his right wrist. He took another step back and I skewered him in the left shoulder. He went over backward.

I looked at the other one, who was big and strong-looking. He showed signs of having been bit in the face by Loiosh. He was swinging his sword wildly over his head while my familiar stayed out of his reach and laughed at him. I spared a quick glance for Bajinok, then, with my left hand, found a knife, aimed, and carefully threw it into the middle of the other guy's stomach. He grunted and cried out and swung in my direction, coming close enough to my wrist to take some hair off my arm. But that was all he had in him. He dropped his sword and knelt on the street, bent over, holding his stomach.

I said, "Okay, get going." I did my best to sound as if I weren't breathing hard.

They looked at each other, then the one with my knife in his stomach teleported out. When he was completely gone, Bajinok stood up and began limping away, holding his injured shoulder. I changed my mind about going straight home. Loiosh continued watching Bajinok as I turned up the street.

"I'd just take it as a warning," said Kragar.

"I don't need you for the obvious stuff."

"I could argue that," he said. "But never mind. The question is, how hard is he going to push it?"

"That," I said, "*is* the kind of stuff I need you for."

"I don't know," he said, "but I assume we're going to get ready for the worst."

I nodded.

"Hey, boss."

"Yeah?"

"Are you going to tell Cawti about this?"

"Huh? Of course I'm going to . . . oh. I see what you mean. When things start to get complicated, they don't go halfway, do they?"

Kragar seemed to have left the room by then, so I took out a dagger and threw it as hard as I could into the wall—the one without a target on it. The gash it left there wasn't the first, but it may have been the deepest.

When I went home a few hours later I still hadn't decided, but Cawti wasn't there. I sat down to wait for her. I was careful not to drink too much. I relaxed in my favorite chair, a big, overstuffed grey thing with a prickly surface that makes me avoid it when I'm unclothed. I spent quite a while relaxing before I began to wonder where Cawti was.

I closed my eyes and concentrated for a moment.

"Yes?"

"Hi. Where are you?"

She paused, and I was suddenly alert. *"Why?"* she said finally.

"Why? Because I want to know. What do you mean, why?"

"I'm in South Adrilankha."

"Are you in any danger?"

"No more than an Easterner is always in danger living in this society."

I bit back a response of *spare me* and said, *"All right. When will you be home?"*

"Why?" she asked and all sorts of prickly things started buzzing around inside of me. I almost said, "I was almost killed today," but it would have been neither true nor fair. So I said *"Never mind"* and severed the link.

I stood up and went into the kitchen. I drew a pot of water and set it on the stove, threw a couple of logs into the stove itself. I stacked up the dishes, which Loiosh and Rocza had already licked clean, and wiped off the table, throwing the crumbs into the stove. I got the broom out and swept the kitchen, threw the refuse from the floor after the crumbs from the table. Then I took the water off the stove and washed the dishes. I used sorcery to dry them because I've always hated drying. When I opened the cupboard to put them away I noticed that it was getting a bit dusty so I took everything out and went over all the shelves with a cloth. I felt the faint stirrings of psionic contact then, but it wasn't Cawti so I ignored it and presently it went away.

I cleaned up the floor below the sink, then mopped the whole floor. I went into the living room, decided I didn't feel like dusting and sat down on the couch. After a couple of minutes I got up, found the brush, and dusted off the shelves next to the door, under the polished wooden dog and the stand with the miniature portrait of Cawti on it, and the carved lyorn that looked like jade but wasn't, and the slightly larger stand with the portrait of my grandfather. I didn't stop and talk to Cawti's portrait.

Then I got a rag from the kitchen and wiped down the tea table that she'd given me last year. I sat down on the couch again.

I noticed that the lyorn's horn was pointing toward Cawti. When she's upset, she can pick the strangest things to think are deliberate, so I got up and turned it, then sat down again. Then I got up and dusted off the *lant* I'd given her last year that she hadn't even tuned in twelve weeks. I walked over to the bookshelf and picked out a book of poems by Wint. I looked at it for a while, then put it back because I didn't feel like fighting with obscurity. I picked up one of Bingia, then decided that she was too depressing. I didn't bother with Torturi or Lartol. I can be shallow and clever on my own; I don't need them for it. I consulted the Orb, then my internal clock, and both told me that I wouldn't be able to sleep yet.

"*Hey, Loiosh.*"

"*Yeah, boss?*"

"*Want to see a show?*"

"*What kind?*"

"*I don't care.*"

"*Sure.*"

I walked over to Kieron Circle instead of teleporting because I didn't care to arrive with my stomach upset. It was a bit of a hike, but walking felt good. I picked a theater without looking at the title, as soon as I found a show that was starting right away. I think it was an historical, taking place during the reign of a decadent Phoenix so they could use all the costumes they had lying around from the last fifty years of productions. After about fifteen minutes I started hoping someone would try to cut my purse. I took a quick glance behind me, and saw an elderly Teckla couple, probably blowing a year's savings. I gave up on that idea.

I left at the end of the first act. Loiosh didn't mind. He didn't think the actor playing the Warlord should have been allowed out of North Hill. He's a real snob when it comes to theater. He said, "*The Warlord is supposed to be a Dragon, boss. Dragons stomp, they don't skulk. And he almost tripped over his sword three times. And when he was supposed to be demanding that more troops be conscripted, it sounded as if he was asking for—*"

"*Which one was the Warlord?*"

He said, "*Oh. Never mind.*"

I walked home slowly, hoping someone would do something to me so I could do something back, but all was quiet in Adrilankha. At one point someone approached me as if he were going to pull on my cloak and I started to get ready for action, but he turned out to be an old, old man, probably an Orca, who was under the influence of something. Before he could open his mouth I asked him if he had any spare copper. He looked confused so I patted his shoulder and walked on.

When we got back, I hung up my cloak, took off my boots and checked the bedroom. Cawti was home and asleep. Rocza was resting in her alcove.

I stood over Cawti, hoping she'd wake up and see me looking at her and ask what was wrong so I could storm at her and she'd apologize and everything would be fine. I stood there for what must have been ten minutes. I might still be standing there, but Loiosh was around. He wasn't saying anything, but he makes me self-conscious about wallowing in self-pity for more than ten minutes at a time, so I undressed and crawled into bed next to Cawti. She didn't wake up. A long, long time later I fell asleep.

I wake up slowly.

Oh, not always. I remember a couple of times when I've woken to Loiosh screaming in my mind and found myself in the middle of a fight. Once or twice I was woken up badly and unfortunate things almost happened, but those are rare. Usually there is a time between awake and asleep that, in retrospect, feels like it lasts for hours. That's when I clutch at my pillow and wonder if I really feel like getting up. Then I roll over, look at the ceiling and the thoughts of what I'm going to do that day trickle into my head. That's what really wakes me up. I've tried to organize my life so that there is something to get up for on any given day. Today we're going to the Eastern section for the spice markets. Today I'm going to close that deal on a new brothel. Today I'm going to visit Castle Black and check on Morrolan's security setup and chat with Aliera. Today

I'm going to follow this guy and confirm that he does visit his mistress every other day. That kind of thing.

When I woke up the next morning, I learned that I was made of better stuff than I had thought, because I got out of bed without having a single reason to. Not one damned reason. Cawti was up, but I didn't know if she was home or not; neither thought gave me any impulse to see the world outside of my room. My business was running itself; I had no obligations to fulfill. The only thing interesting in my life was finding out the story behind who had killed the Easterner, and that was for Cawti, who seemed not to care.

But I made it into the kitchen to start heating water. Cawti was in the living room reading a tabloid. I felt a tightening in my throat. I started the water, then went into the bathroom. I used the chamber pot and cleaned it with sorcery. Neat. Efficient. Just like a Dragaeran. I shaved in cold water. My grandfather shaved in cold water (before he grew his beard) because he says it makes you better able to stand the winters. That sounds like nonsense to me, but I do it out of respect for him. I chewed on a tooth stick, rubbed down my gums, and rinsed my mouth out. By then the water was hot enough for my bath. I took it, dried myself, cleaned up the bathroom, dressed, and dumped the water out the back. Splash. I stood and watched the puddles and rivers it made running down the alley. I've often wondered why no one claims to read the future in dumped bath water. I looked to the left and saw the ground was dry beneath my neighbor's back porch. Ha! I was up earlier than she again. So there, world. One small victory.

I walked into the living room and sat down in my chair, facing the couch. I caught a glimpse of a headline on Cawti's tabloid that read, "Call for the investigation—" on about four lines of big black print, and that wasn't the whole thing. She put the thing down and looked at me.

I said, "I'm mad at you."

She said, "I know. Should we go out and eat?"

I nodded. For some reason, we can't seem to discuss things at home. We went to our favorite klava hole with Loiosh and Rocza on my shoulders and I ignored the tension and twisting in my stomach long enough to order a few eggs and drink some klava with very little honey. Cawti ordered tea.

She said, "Okay. Why are you mad?" which is like getting in the first cut to put the other guy on the defensive.

So I said, "Why didn't you tell me where you were?"

She said, "Why did you want to know?" with a bit of a smile as we realized what we were doing.

I said, "Why shouldn't I?" and we both grinned, and I felt just a little better for just a little while.

Then she shook her head and said, "When you asked where I was and when I'd be back, it sounded as if you wanted to approve or disapprove of it."

I felt my head snap back. "That's absurd," I said. "I just wanted to know where you were."

She glared at me. "All right, so I'm absurd. That still doesn't give you the right—"

"Dammit, I didn't say *you* were absurd and you know it. You're accusing me—"

"I didn't accuse you of anything. I said how I felt."

"Well, by saying that you felt that way, you were implying that—"

"This is ridiculous."

Which was the perfect chance to say, "All right, so I'm ridiculous," but I know better. Instead, I said, "Look, I was not then trying, nor have I ever tried, to dictate your actions. I came home, you weren't there—"

"Oh, and this is the first time that's happened?"

"Yes," I said, which we both knew wasn't true, but the word came out before I could stop it. The corner of her mouth twitched up and the eyebrow lowered, which is one of my favorite things that she does. "All right," I said. "But I was worried about you."

"About me?" she said. "Or afraid that I was involved in something you don't approve of?"

"I already know you're involved in something I don't approve of."

"Why don't you approve of it?"

I said, "Because it's *stupid*, first of all. How are five Easterners and a Teckla going to 'destroy the despotism' of an Empire? And—"

"There are more. That's only the tip of the iceberg."

I stopped. "What's an iceberg?"

"Ummm . . . I don't know. You know what I mean."

"Yeah. The thing is, it's not even nearing a Teckla reign. I could see something like this if the Teckla were near the top of the Cycle, but they're not. It's the Phoenix, and then the Dragons if we're still alive when the Cycle changes; the Teckla aren't even in the running.

"And in the second place, what's wrong with what we have now? Of course it isn't perfect, but we live well enough and we got it on our own. You're talking about giving up our careers, our life-style, and everything else. And for what? So a bunch of nobodies can pretend they're important—"

"Careful," she said.

I stopped in mid-diatribe. "All right," I said. "Sorry. But have I answered your question?"

She was quiet for a long time, then. Our food showed up and we ate it without saying anything at all. When we'd turned the scraps over to Loiosh and Rocza, Cawti said, "Vladimir, we've always agreed never to hit each other's weak spots, right?"

I felt a sinking sensation when she said that, but I nodded.

She continued, "All right, this is going to sound like that's what I'm doing, but I don't mean it that way, okay?"

"Go on," I said.

She shook her head. "Is it okay? I want to say it, because I think it's important, but I don't want you to just shut me out, the way you do whenever I try to get you to look at yourself. So will you listen?"

I drained my klava, signaled the waiter for more and doctored it appropriately when it came. "All right," I said.

"Until just recently," she began, "you thought that you had found your line of work because you hated Dragaerans. Killing them was your way of getting back at them for what they'd put you through while you were growing up. Right?"

I nodded.

"Okay," she continued. "A few weeks ago, you had a talk with Aliera."

I winced. "Yeah," I said.

"She told you about a previous life in which—"

"Yeah, I know. I was a Dragaeran."

"And you said you felt as if your whole life had been a lie."

"Yes."

"Why?"

"Hm?"

"Why did it shake you so much?"

"I don't—"

"Could it be because you've felt all along as if you had to justify yourself? Could it be that somewhere, deep down, you think it is *evil* to kill people for money?"

"Not people," I said by reflex. "Dragaerans."

"People," she said. "And I think you've just proved my point. You were forced into this line of work, just the way I was. You had to justify it to yourself. You've justified it so thoroughly that you kept on doing 'work' even after you no longer had to, when you were making enough money from running your area that the 'work' was pointless. And then your justification fell apart. So now you don't know where you stand, and you have to wonder whether you are, really, deep down, a bad person."

"I don't—"

"Let me finish. What I'm getting at is this: No, you *aren't* a bad person. You have done what you had to do to live and to help provide us both with a home and a comfortable life. But tell me this, now that you can't hide behind hating Dragaerans any more: What kind of Empire do we have that forces someone like you to do what you do, just to live, and to be able to walk down the streets without flinching? What kind of Empire not only produces the Jhereg, but allows it to thrive? Can you justify *that*?"

I let her comments percolate through me for a while. I got more klava. Then I said, "That's the way things are. Even if these people you're running around with *aren't* just nut cases, nothing they do is going to change that. Put in a different Emperor and things will just go back to being the way they are in a few years. Sooner than that, if it's an Easterner."

"That," she said, "is a whole 'nother subject. The point I'm making is that you're going to have to come to terms with what you do, at whose expense you live, and why. I'll help as much as I can, but it is your own life you have to deal with."

I stared into my klava cup. Nothing in it made anything any clearer.

After another cup or two I said, "All right, but you still haven't told me where you were."

She said, "I was conducting a class."

"A class? On what?"

"Reading. For a group of Easterners and Teckla."

I stared at her. "My wife, the teacher."

"Don't."

"Sorry."

Then I said, "How long have you been doing this?"

"I just started."

"Oh. Well." I cleared my throat. "How did it go?"

"Fine."

"Oh." Then another, nastier thought occurred to me. "Why is it only now that you've started doing this?"

"Someone had to take over for Franz," she said, confirming exactly what I was afraid of.

"I see. Has it occurred to you that this may be what he'd been doing that someone didn't like? That this was why he was killed?"

She looked straight at me. "Yes."

A chill spread along my backbone. "So you're asking—"

"I'm not Franz."

"Anyone can be killed, Cawti. As long as someone is willing to pay a professional—and it's clear that someone is—*anyone* can be killed. You know that."

"Yes," she said.

"No," I said.

"No what?"

"Don't. Don't make me choose—"

"*I* am choosing."

"I can't let you walk into a situation where you're a helpless target."

"You can't stop me."

"I can. I don't know how yet, but I can."

"If you do, I'll leave you."

"You won't have that choice if you're dead."

She paused to wipe up the klava that had spilled from my cup. "We are not helpless, you know. We have support."

"Of Easterners. Of Teckla."

"It is the Teckla who feed everyone else."

"I know. And I know what happens to them when they try to do anything about it. There have been revolts, you know. There has never been a successful one except during the reign of the Orca, right before the Teckla. As I said, we aren't there now."

"We're not discussing a Teckla revolt. We're not talking about a Teckla reign; we're talking about breaking the Cycle itself."

"Adron tried that once; remember? He destroyed a city and caused an interregnum that lasted more than two hundred years, and it still didn't work."

"We aren't doing it with pre-Empire sorcery, or magic of any kind. We're doing it with the strength of the masses—the ones who have the *real* power."

I withheld my opinion of what real power is and who has it. I said, "I can't allow you to be killed, Cawti. I just can't."

"The best way to protect me would be to join us. We could use—"

"Words," I said. "Nothing but words."

"Yes," said Cawti. "Words from the minds and hearts of thinking human beings. There is no more powerful force in the world, nor a better weapon, once they are applied."

"Pretty," I said. "But I can't accept it."

"You'll have to. Or, at least, you'll have to confront it."

I didn't answer. I was thinking. We didn't say any more, but before we left the klava hole I knew what I was going to have to do. Cawti wasn't going to like it.

But then, neither was I.

4 =

1 pr grey trousers:
remove bloodstain from upper right leg. . .

Just in case I haven't made it clear yet, the walk over to
the Easterners' section takes a good two hours. I was
getting sick of it. Or maybe not. Now that I think back
on it, I could have teleported in three seconds, then
spent fifteen or twenty minutes throwing up or wishing I
could. So I guess maybe I wanted the time to walk and
think. But I remember thinking that I was spending
altogether too much time just walking back and forth
between the Malak Circle district and South Adrilankha.

But I made it there. I entered the building and stood
outside the doorway, which now had a curtain. I
remembered not to clap, and I didn't feel like pounding
on the wall, so I called out, "Is anyone in there?"

There was a sound of footsteps, the curtain moved
and I was looking at my friend Gregory. Sheryl was
behind him, watching me. I couldn't tell if anyone else
was in the room. Since it was Gregory who was standing
there, I brushed past him and said, "Is Kelly around?"

"Come right in," said Sheryl. I felt a little embar-
rassed. No one else was in the room. In one corner was a

47

tall stack of tabloids, the same one Cawti had been reading.

Gregory said, "Why do you want to see him?"

"I plan to leave all my worldly wealth to the biggest idiot I can find and I wanted to interview him to see if he qualified. But now that I've met you, I can see there's no point in looking any further."

He glared at me. Sheryl laughed a little and Gregory flushed.

Kelly appeared through the curtain then. I looked at him more closely than I had before. He really was quite overweight, as well as short, but I somehow wanted to call him extremely chubby instead of fat. Cute, sort of. His forehead was flat, giving the impression that his head was large. His hair was cut very short, like half an inch, and he had no sideburns at all. His eyes had two positions, narrowed and squinting, and he had a very expressive mouth, probably because of the amount of fat surrounding it. He struck me as one of those people who can turn from cheerful to vicious in an instant; like Glowbug, say.

He said, "Right. Come on." Then he turned and walked toward the rear of the flat, leaving me to follow him. I wondered if that was a deliberate ploy.

The back room was narrow and stuffy and smelled of pipe smoke, although Kelly didn't have the teeth of a smoker. Come to think of it, he probably didn't have any vices at all. Except overeating, anyway. Shame he was an Easterner. Dragaerans can use sorcery to remove excess fat; Easterners tend to kill themselves trying. There were rows of leather-bound books all around the room, with black or sometimes brown bindings. I couldn't read any of the titles, but the author of one of them was Padraic Kelly.

He nodded me into a stiff wooden chair and sat in another one behind a rickety-looking desk. I pointed to the book and said, "You wrote that?"

He followed my pointing finger. "Yes."

"What is it?"

"It's a history of the uprising of two twenty-one."

"Where was that?"

He looked at me closely, as if to see if I were joking, then said, "Right here, in South Adrilankha."

I said, "Oh." I cleared my throat. "Do you read poetry as well?"

"Yes," he said.

I sighed to myself. I didn't really want to walk in and start haranguing him, but there didn't seem to be a whole lot else to talk about. What's the use? I said, "Cawti's been telling me something about what you do." He nodded, waiting. "I don't like it," I said, and his eyes narrowed. "I'm not happy that Cawti's involved." He kept staring at me, not saying anything.

I sat back in the chair, crossed my legs. "But all right. I don't run her life. If she wants to waste her time this way, there's nothing I can do about it." I paused, waiting for him to make some sort of interjection. When he didn't, I said, "What bothers me is this business of teaching reading classes—that's what Franz was doing, wasn't it?"

"That, and other things," he said, tight-lipped.

"Well then, I'm offering you a deal. I'll find out who killed Franz and why, if you drop these classes, or get someone else to teach them."

He never took his eyes off me. "And if not?"

I started to get irritated, probably because he was making me feel uncomfortable and I don't like that. I clenched my teeth together, stifling the urge to say what I thought of him. I finally said, "Don't make me threaten you. I dislike threatening people."

He leaned over the desk, and his eyes were narrowed more than usual, his lips were pressed tightly together. He said, "You come in here, on the heels of the death of a man who was martyred to—"

"Spare me."

"Quiet! I said martyred and I meant it. He was fighting for what he believed in, and he was killed for it."

He stared hard at me for a moment, then he continued in a tone of voice that was softer but cutting. "I know what you do for a living," he said. "You don't even realize the depths to which you've sunk."

I touched the hilt of a dagger but didn't draw it. "You're right," I said. "I don't realize the depths to which I've sunk. It would be really stupid of you to tell me about it."

"Don't tell me what is and is not stupid. You're incapable of judging that, or anything else that falls outside the experience of your tiny world. It doesn't even occur to you that there could be anything *wrong* with selling death as if it were any commodity on the market."

"No," I said. "It doesn't. And if you're quite finished—"

"But it isn't just you. Think of this, Lord Killer: How much of what anyone does is something he'd do willingly, if he didn't have to? You accept that without thinking about it or questioning it, don't you? While Easterners and Teckla are forced to sell half their children to feed the rest. You think it doesn't happen, or do you just refuse to look at it?"

He shook his head, and I could see his teeth were clenched in his jowls and his eyes were so narrow I'm surprised he could see out of them. "What you do—mankind doesn't get any lower. I don't know if you do it because you have no choice, or because you've been so twisted that you like it, but it doesn't matter. In this building you will find men and women who can be proud of what they do, because they know there will be a better future for it. And you, with your snide, cynical wit, not only refuse to look at it, but try to tell us how to go about it. We have no time for you or for your deals. And your threats don't impress us either."

He paused, maybe to see if I had anything to say. I didn't.

He said, "Get out of here."

I stood up and left.

"The difference between winning and losing is whether you feel like going home afterwards."

"Not bad, boss. So where are we going?"

"I don't know."

"We could go back to Herth's place, spit in his soup and see what he says about that."

I didn't think this was at all a good idea.

It was still afternoon, and the Easterners' section was in full swing. There were markets every few blocks, and each was different. This one was yellow, orange, red, and green with vegetables and smelled like fresh things and the sound was a low hum. That one was pale and pink and smelled of meat, most of it still good, and it was quieter, so you could even hear the wind rattling around inside your ear. The next one was mostly fabrics and the loudest, because no one bargains like a fabric merchant, with screams and yells and pleading. They don't ever seem to tire of it, either. I get tired of things. I get tired of lots of things. I get tired of walking around Morrolan's castle to check up on his guards, traps, and alarms. I get tired of talking to my associates in codes that even I don't understand half the time. I get tired of breaking out in a sweat every time I see the uniform of the Phoenix Guards. I get tired of being treated with contempt for being a Jhereg by other Houses, and for being an Easterner by Jhereg. And I was getting tired, every time I thought of Cawti, of a tightening in my middle instead of that warm, dropping, glowing feeling I used to have.

"You have to find an answer, boss."

"I know. I just tried."

"So try something else."

"Yeah."

I found that I had wandered over to the area near where my grandfather lived, which couldn't have been an accident although it felt like one. I walked through his doorway and set the chimes ringing. They were cheerful. I actually started feeling better as I stepped over the threshold. Chimes. Now, there's a witch for you.

He was sitting at his table, writing or drawing with a quill pen on a big piece of parchment. He was old, but very healthy. A big man. If Kelly was chubby, my grandfather was portly. His head was almost completely bald, so it reflected the little lamps of the shop. He looked up when he heard the chimes and gave me a big grin with his remaining teeth.

"Vladimir!"

"Hello, Noish-pa."

We hugged and he kissed my cheek. Loiosh flew off my shoulder onto a shelf until we were done, then flew to Noish-pa's arm for some chin-scratching. His familiar, a large furry cat named Ambrus, jumped into my lap when I sat down and poked his nose at me. We got reacquainted. Noish-pa hooked a small card onto the string that held the chimes and motioned me into his back room. I smelled herb tea and started feeling even better.

He served us, *tsk*ing when I put honey in mine. I sipped it. Rose hip.

"So, how is my grandson?"

"So-so, I guess, Noish-pa."

"Only so-so?"

I nodded.

"You have a problem," he said.

"Yeah. It's complicated."

"Simple things are never problems, Vladimir. Some simple things are sad, but never problems."

"Yeah."

"So, how did this problem start?"

"How did it start? Someone named Franz was killed."

"Ah! Yes. A terrible thing."

I stared at him. "You know about it?"

"It is on everyone's tongue."

"It is?"

"Well, these people, his . . . what is the word? *Elvtarsok*?"

"Friends? Associates?"

"Well, these people are everywhere, and they talk about it."

"I see."

"But you, Vladimir. You are not one of these people, are you?"

I shook my head. "Cawti is."

He sighed. "Vlad, Vlad, Vlad. It is silliness. If a revolution comes along, of course you support it. But to go out of your way like this is to put your head on the block."

"When has revolution come along?"

"Eh? In two twenty-one."

"Oh. Yes. Of course."

"Yes. We fought then, because it was what we did, but some can't forget that and think we should be always fighting."

I said, "What do you know about these people?"

"Oh, I hear things. Their leader, this Kelly, he is a fighter they say."

"A fighter? A brawler?"

"No, no. I mean he never quits, that is what I hear. And they are getting bigger, you know. I remember I heard of them a few years ago when they had a parade of twenty people, and now they have thousands."

"Why do people go there?"

"Oh, there are always those who aren't happy. And there has been violence here; beatings and robbing of people, and they say the Phoenix Guards of the Empire don't stop it. And some landlords raise their rent because some of their houses burn down, and people are unhappy about that, too."

"But none of that has anything to do with Cawti. We don't even live around here."

He shook his head and *tsk*ed. "It is silliness," he repeated.

I said, "What can I do?"

He shrugged. "Your grandmother did things I didn't like, Vladimir. There is nothing to be done. Perhaps she will lose interest." He frowned. "No, that is unlikely. Cawti does not lose interest when she becomes interested. But there, it is her life, not yours."

"But Noish-pa, that's just it. It's her *life*. Someone killed this Franz, and now Cawti is doing just what he was doing. If she wants to run around with these people and stir up trouble, or whatever they're doing, that's fine, but if she were killed, I couldn't stand it. But I can't stop her, or she'll leave me."

He frowned again and nodded. "Have you tried things?"

"Yes. I tried talking to Kelly, but that didn't do anything."

"Do you know who it was who killed this Franz fellow?"

"Yeah, I know who."

"And why?"

I paused. "No, I don't really know that."

"Then you must find out. Perhaps you will find that there is nothing to worry about, after all. If there is, perhaps you will find a way to solve it without risk to your wife."

Your wife he said. Not *Cawti* this time, it was *your wife*. That was how he thought. Family. Everything was family, and we were all the family he had. It suddenly occurred to me that he was probably disappointed in me; I don't think he approved of assassins, but I was family so that was that.

"What do you think of my work, Noish-pa?"

He shook his head. "It is terrible, what you do. It is not good for a man to live by killing. It hurts you."

"Okay." I was sorry I had asked. I said, "Thank you, Noish-pa. I have to go now."

"It was good to see you again, Vladimir."

I hugged him, collected Loiosh, and walked out of his shop. The way back to my side of town was long, and I still didn't feel like teleporting.

When Cawti came home that evening, I was soaking my feet.

"What's the matter?" she asked.

"My feet hurt."

She gave me a half-smile. "Somehow this doesn't surprise me. I mean, *why* do your feet hurt?''

''I've been walking a lot the last few days.''

She sat down across from me and stretched out. She was wearing high-waisted grey slacks with a wide black belt, a grey jerkin and a black vest. She'd hung up her half-cloak. ''Anywhere in particular?''

''The Easterners' section, mostly.''

She turned her head to the side a bit, which was one of my favorite things to see her do. It made her eyes seem huge in that beautiful, thin face with her perfectly sculpted cheekbones. ''Doing what?''

''I went in to see Kelly.''

Her eyes widened. ''Why?''

''I explained that he should make sure you weren't doing anything that might put you in danger. I implied that I'd kill him if he did.''

The look of curiosity changed to disbelief, then anger. ''Did you really,'' she said.

''Yeah.''

''You don't seem nervous about telling me about it.''

''Thank you.''

''And what did Kelly say?''

''He said that, as a human being, I rated somewhere between worthless scum and wretched garbage.''

She looked startled. Not upset, startled. ''He said that?''

''Not in so many words. Quite.''

''Hmmm,'' she said.

''I'm glad to see that this outrage against your husband fills you with such a righteous indignation.''

''Hmmm,'' she said.

''Trying to decide if he was right?''

''Oh, no,'' she said. ''I know he's right. I was wondering how he could tell.''

''Cawti—'' I said, and stopped because my voice broke.

She came over, sat beside me, and put her hand on my leg. ''I'm sorry,'' she said. ''I didn't mean that and I shouldn't have joked about it. I know he's wrong. But you shouldn't have done what you did.''

"I know," I said, almost whispering.

We were silent for a time. She said, "What are you going to do now?"

"I think," I said, "that I'm going to wait until my feet feel better. Then I'm going to go out and kill someone."

She stared at me. "Are you serious?"

"Yes. No. I'm not sure. Half, I guess."

"This is hard for you. I'm sorry."

I nodded.

She said, "It's going to get harder."

"Yeah."

"I wish I could help you."

"You have. You'd do more if you could."

She nodded. After that there wasn't any more to say, so she just sat next to me for a while. Presently, we went into the bedroom and slept.

I was in the office early the next morning, with Loiosh and Rocza. I let them out my window so Loiosh could continue showing Rocza around. He had gradually been teaching her the ins and outs of the city. He enjoyed it, too. I wondered what that would do to a marriage—one having to train the other. With those two it could become strained, too—Loiosh did the teaching, but the jhereg female is dominant.

"Hey, Loiosh—"

"None of your Verra-be-damned business, boss."

That was hardly fair; he'd been butting into *my* marriage. Besides, I had a right to know if I was going to be subjected to more cheap North Hill theater than what I was generating. But I didn't push it.

By the time they returned, a couple of hours later, I knew what I was going to do. I got an address from Kragar, along with a dirty look for not telling him why I wanted it. Loiosh and Rocza attached themselves to my shoulders and I went down the stairs and out of the office.

Lower Kieron Road, near Malak Circle, is the widest

street in this part of town and is filled with inns set back from it and markets jutting out into it and hotels, some with small businesses inside of them. I owned all the small businesses. Lower Kieron took me south and west. It got gradually narrower, and more and more tenements appeared. Most of them had once been green but were now painted dirty. I abandoned Lower Kieron to follow a narrow little street called Ulor.

Ulor widened after a bit, and about there I turned onto Copper Street, which was different from the Copper Lane near my place, or the Copper Street to the east or the Copper Street even further east or the others that I don't remember. After a few paces, I turned left into a fairly nice looking inn with long tables of polished wood and long benches. I found the host and said, "Do you have a private room?"

He allowed as to how he did, although his look implied it wasn't normally polluted by the presence of Easterners. I said, "My name is Vlad. Tell Bajinok that I'm here."

He nodded and called for a serving man to carry the message. I spotted where the back room must be and entered it. It was empty. I was pleased that it had a real door. I closed it and sat, back to the door (Loiosh was watching), on one of the benches at a table that was a shorter version of the ones in the main room. I wondered how many people Bajinok would bring along. If it was more than one, this probably wouldn't work. But then, he might not bring anyone. I decided I had pretty good odds.

Presently, the door opened and Bajinok came in along with another Jhereg I hadn't seen before. I stood up before they could sit down.

"Good morning," I said. "I hope I didn't disturb you."

Bajinok scowled a little. "What?" he said.

"A man of few words," I told him. "I like that." Loiosh hissed, which he might have thought was agreement.

"What do you want?"

"I thought we might continue our discussion of the other day."

The Jhereg who was with Bajinok rolled his shoulders and scratched his stomach. Bajinok wiped his hands on his cloak. I checked the clasp of my cloak with one hand and brushed my hair back with the other. I didn't know about them, but all of *my* weapons were ready.

He said, "If you have something to say, say it."

"I want to know why Herth wanted that Easterner killed."

Bajinok said, "Drop dead, whiskers."

I gestured with my right hand as if I were about to say something important. I suppose in a way I was. The gesture produced a dagger that went straight up under the unknown's chin and into his head. He crumbled, fell against me and slid to the floor. By the time he hit, I had taken another dagger from my cloak and was holding the point of it directly in front of Bajinok's left eye.

I said, "The instant anyone appears in this room, or opens the door, or you even look like you're in psionic communication with someone, I'm going to kill you."

He said, "Okay."

"I thought you might want to tell me a few things about Herth and why he wanted that Easterner killed."

Without moving his head, he glanced down at the corpse. Then he looked back up the blade of the dagger. "You know," he said, "I just might at that."

"Good," I said cheerfully.

"Mind if I sit down?"

"No. Go ahead."

He did, and I moved behind him and held my blade against the back of his neck. He said, "This is going to get you killed, you know."

"We all have to die sometime. And we Easterners don't live that long anyway. Of course, that's a good reason not to rush things, I suppose. Which brings us back to Franz." I increased the pressure against the back of his neck. I felt him flinch. I stayed alert for any attempt to teleport out. I could kill him before he was gone if I was quick.

He said, "Yes. Franz. He was a member of some kind of group—"

"I know about it."

"Okay. Then there isn't much more I can tell you."

I pressed the knife against his neck again. "Try. Were you told to kill him in particular, or just some member of the group?"

"I was given his name."

"Have you been keeping tabs on what these people have been doing?"

"Herth has."

"I know that, idiot. I mean, are you the one who's been watching them?"

"No."

"Who is?"

"A fellow named Nath."

"Where can I find him?"

"Are you going to kill me?"

"Not if you keep talking."

"He lives above a carpetmaker way to the west, just north of the Easterners' area. Number four Shade Tree Street."

I said, "Okay. Do you plan to tell Herth about this talk?"

"Yes."

"You'll have to tell him what you told me."

"He's very understanding that way."

"In that case, I need a good reason for leaving you alive."

"You said you would."

"Yes, that is a good reason. I need another one."

"You're a dead man, you know."

"I know."

"A dishonest dead man."

"I'm just in a bad mood. I'm usually a very honest dead man. Ask anyone."

"Okay. I'll keep my mouth shut for an hour."

"Would you keep your word to someone who lied to you?"

He considered that for a moment, then said, "Yes."

"Herth must be a very understanding fellow."

"Yes. Except when his people are killed. He doesn't understand that at all."

I said, "Okay. You can leave."

He stood up without another word and walked out. I replaced my dagger, left the one in the body and walked back out into the main room. The host didn't give me a second glance. I made it onto the street and headed back toward my office. I could feel Loiosh's tension as he strained to look into every corner of every alley we passed.

"You shouldn't have killed that guy, boss."

"If I hadn't, Bajinok wouldn't have taken me seriously. And I'm not certain I could have controlled two of them."

"Herth will be after your head now."

"Yes."

"You can't help Cawti if you're dead."

"I know."

"Then why—"

"Shut up."

Even I didn't think that was much of an answer.

5 –

. . .klava stain from upper left. . .

I teleported to a place I knew in Nath's neighborhood, so I wouldn't have to waste any of Bajinok's hour. Then I wasted a good fifteen minutes while my stomach recovered from the teleport.

Shade Tree Street must have been an old name. There were a few stumps in the ground to the sides, and the hotels and houses were set back quite a ways from the crude stonework curbing on either edge of the street itself, which was as wide as Lower Kieron. The width indicated that the area had once had a lot of shops and markets, and that later it had been one of the better sections of town. That was probably before the Interregnum, however. Now it was a little on the low side.

Number four was right in the middle, between number fifteen and number six. It was of brown stonework, two stories tall, with two flats in it. The one on the bottom had a chreotha crudely drawn on the door. I went up the wooden steps and they didn't creak at all. I was impressed.

The door at the top had a stylized jhereg on it, etched on a metal plate above the symbol for Baron. *"Was I quiet enough, Loiosh?"*

"I think so, boss."

"Okay."

I checked the spells on the door, then checked them a second time. I'm a lot sloppier when I'm not actually about to kill someone, but there's no reason to be *too* sloppy. The door held no surprises. The wood itself was thin enough that I could handle it. I let Spellbreaker fall into my left hand, took a couple of careful breaths, then smacked the door with Spellbreaker and, at the same time, kicked with my right leg. The door flew open and I stepped into the room.

He was alone. That meant it was likely that Bajinok had actually kept his word. He was sitting on a low couch, reading the same tabloid that Cawti had been reading. I kicked the door shut behind me and crossed to him in three steps, drawing my rapier as I did so. He stood up and stared at me, wide-eyed. He made no effort to reach for a weapon. It was possible he wasn't a fighter, but it would be stupid to count on it. I held the point of my weapon up to his left eye and said, "Good afternoon. You must be Nath."

He stared at me, his eyes wide, holding his breath.

I said, "Well?"

He nodded.

I gave him the same speech I'd given Bajinok about not leaving or trying to reach help. He seemed to find it convincing. I said, "Let's sit down and chat."

He nodded again. He was either very frightened or a good actor. I said, "An Easterner named Franz was killed a few days ago."

He nodded.

I said, "Herth had it done."

He nodded again.

I said, "You pointed him out to Herth."

His eyes widened and he half-shook his head.

I said, "Yes. Why?"

"I didn't—"

"I don't care if you suggested the killing or not. I want to know what it was about Franz that you told Herth. Tell me quickly, without thinking about it. If I get the idea that you're lying, I'll kill you."

His mouth worked for a bit, and his voice, when he spoke, was a squeak. "I don't know. I just—" he stopped long enough to clear his throat. "I just told him about them. All of them. I said what they were doing."

"Herth wanted to know names?"

"Not at first. But a few weeks ago he told me to give him reports on all of the Easterners—their names, what they did, everything."

"You had all that?"

He nodded.

I asked, "Why?"

"I've been here for most of the year. Herth heard rumors about this group and sent me to check on them. I've been keeping track."

"I see. And then he tells you to give him the names, and two weeks later Franz is killed."

He nodded.

I said, "Well, why did he want someone killed, and why Franz?"

He said, "I don't know."

"Guess."

"They were troublemakers. They interfered with business. They were always around, you know? And they were giving reading lessons. When Easterners—" He stopped, looking at me.

"Go on."

He swallowed. "When Easterners get too smart, well, I guess it doesn't help business any. But it might have been something that happened before I came. Herth is careful, you know? He wouldn't tell me more than he had to."

"And Franz?"

"He was just one of them."

"What about Kelly?"

"What about him? He never did much that I could see."

I refrained from commenting on his eyesight.

"Boss."

"Yeah, Loiosh?"

"Your hour is about gone."

"Thanks."

I said, "Okay. You get to live."

He seemed relieved. I turned, walked out the door and down to the street and made my way through some alleys as quickly as I could. There was no sign of pursuit.

"Well, what do you think, Loiosh?"

"He wanted to kill one of them, and Franz was as good a choice as any."

"Yeah. I think so, too. Why did he want to kill one of them?"

"I don't know."

"Well, what now?"

"Boss, do you have an idea how much trouble you've gotten yourself into?"

"Yeah."

"I was just wondering. I don't know what to do now, boss. We're close to the Easterners' area, if there's anything you want there."

I started heading that way as I thought about it. What was the next step? I had to find out if Herth was going to keep after them now, or if he had accomplished whatever it was he hoped to accomplish. If Herth wasn't going to do anything to these people, I could relax and only worry about how I was going to keep him from killing me.

The street I was on dead-ended unexpectedly, so I backtracked a ways until I found one I knew. Tall, windowless houses loomed over me like gloating green and yellow giants, with balconies sometimes almost meeting above me, cutting off my view of the orange-red sky.

Then, at a cross street named Twovine, the houses became older, paler, and smaller and the street widened and I was in the Easterners' section. It smelled like the countryside, with hay and cows and manure where they were selling cow's milk on the street. The breeze became sharper with the widening of the avenue, in swirls that kicked dust up in my eyes and stung my face.

The street curved and twisted and others joined it and left it, and then I saw Sheryl and Paresh standing on a street corner, holding that same damned tabloid and accosting passers-by. I walked up to them. Paresh nodded coolly and turned his back to me. Sheryl's smile was a little friendlier, but she also turned away when two young Easterners came by, holding hands. I heard her saying something about breaking the Imperium, but they just shook their heads and walked on.

I said, "Am I off limits?"

Sheryl shook her head. Paresh turned and said, "Not at all. Do you want to buy a copy?"

I said I didn't. He didn't seem surprised. He turned away again. I stood there for a few more seconds before realizing that I was making a fool of myself by standing, and I'd look stupid leaving. I addressed Sheryl. "Will you talk to me if I buy you a cup of klava?"

"I can't," she said. "Since Franz was murdered we don't work alone."

I bit my tongue when a few remarks about "working" came to mind, then got an idea.

"Well, Loiosh?"

"Oh, sure boss. Why not?"

I said to Sheryl, "Loiosh can stick around."

She looked startled and glanced at Paresh. Paresh looked at Loiosh for a moment, then said, "Why not?"

So Loiosh hung around and got his revolutionary indoctrination while I led Sheryl into an Easterner klava hole located right across the street. It was long, narrow, darker than I like except when I want to kill someone; everything was of wood in surprisingly good condition, considering. I led us all the way to the far end and put my back to the wall. That isn't really a useful way of protecting yourself, but on that occasion it made me feel better.

I had promised to buy her a cup of klava, but actually it came in a glass. I burned my hand on the side when I first picked it up, then, setting it down, slopped some onto the table and burned my leg. I put cream in to cool it down, which didn't help much because they warmed the cream. Tasted good though.

Sheryl's eyes were wide and bright blue, with just a

hint of freckles around them. I said, "You know what I'm doing?"

"Not exactly," she said. There was the hint of a smile about her lips. It suddenly occurred to me that she might think I was making a pass at her. Then it occurred to me that maybe I wanted to. She was certainly attractive, and had a bit of the innocent wanton about her that I found stimulating. But no, not now.

I said, "I'm trying to find out why Franz was killed, and then I'm going to do whatever I have to to make sure that Cawti isn't."

The almost-smile didn't waver, but she shook her head. "Franz was killed because they're scared of us."

There were a lot of snappy answers that I didn't make. Instead I said, "Who is scared?"

"The Imperium."

"He wasn't killed by the Imperium."

"Perhaps not directly, but—"

"He was killed by a Jhereg named Herth. Herth doesn't kill people for the Imperium. He's too busy trying to keep the Imperium from finding out that he kills people."

"It may look like that—"

"All right, all right. This isn't helping."

She shrugged, and by now the smile was gone. On the other hand, she wasn't looking angry, so it was worth continuing. I said, "What was he doing, in particular, that would threaten a Jhereg trying to make money, in particular?"

She was quiet for a while, and at last said, "I don't know. He sold papers, just as I was doing, and he spoke at meetings, just as I do, and he gave lessons on reading, and on revolution, just as I do—"

"Wait. You also give reading lessons?"

"We all do."

"I see. All right."

"I guess what it was is that he did more of everything. He was tireless, and enthusiastic, and everyone responded to that—both we, and people we'd run across. When we'd travel through the neighborhoods, he al-

ways remembered people better than the rest of us, and
they always remembered him. When he spoke, he was
better. When he gave reading lessons, it was like it was
vital to him that everyone learned to read. Whenever
some group that I was in was doing something, he was
always there, and whenever some group that I *wasn't* in
was doing something, he was always there, too. Do you
see what I mean?"

I nodded and didn't say anything. The waiter came
and poured more klava. I added cream and honey and
used the napkin to hold the glass. Glass. Why not a cup?
Stupid Easterners; can't do anything right.

I said, "Do you know any of the Jhereg who operate
around here?"

She shook her head. "I know there are some, but I
wouldn't recognize them. There are a good number of
Dragaerans, and a lot of them are Jhereg, but I couldn't
tell you 'that guy works for the organization,' or
something."

"Do you know what kind of things they have going
on?"

"No, not really."

"Are there places to gamble?"

"Huh? Oh, sure. But they're run by Easterners."

"No, they're not."

"How do you know?"

"I know Herth."

"Oh."

"Are there prostitutes?"

"Yes."

"Brothels?"

"Yes."

"Pimps?"

She suddenly looked, perhaps, the least bit smug.
"Not any more," she said.

"Ah ha."

"What?"

"What happened to them?"

"We drove them off. They're the most vicious—"

"I know pimps. How did you drive them off?"

"Most of the pimps around here were really young kids."

"Yes. The older ones run brothels."

"They were part of the gangs."

"Gangs?"

"Yes. Around here there isn't much of anything for kids to do, so—"

"How old kids?"

"Oh, you know, eleven to sixteen."

"Okay."

"So they formed gangs, just to have something to do. And they'd wander around and make trouble, break up stores, that kind of thing. Your Phoenix Guards couldn't care less about what they do, as long as they stay in our area."

"They aren't *my* Phoenix Guards."

"Whatever. There have been gangs around here for longer than I've been alive. A lot of them get involved in pimping because it's about the only way to make money when you don't have any money to start with. They also terrorize a lot of the small shopkeepers into paying them, and steal a little, but there just isn't that much to steal and no one to sell it to."

I suddenly thought about Noish-pa, but no, they wouldn't mess around with a witch. I said, "Okay, so some of them got into pimping."

"Yes."

"How did you get rid of them?"

"Kelly says that most of the kids in the gangs are in because they don't have any hope of things being better for them. He says that their only real hope is revolution, so—"

"Fine," I said. "How did you get rid of them?"

"We broke up most of the gangs."

"How?"

"We taught them to read, for one thing. Once you can read it's harder to remain ignorant. And when they saw we were serious about destroying the despots, many of them joined us."

"Just like that?"

For the first time she glared at me. "It's taken us ten years of work to get this far, and we still have a long way to go. Ten years. It wasn't 'just like that.' And not all of them stayed in the movement, either. But, so far, most of the gangs are gone and haven't come back."

"And when the gangs broke up, the pimps left?"

"They needed the gangs to back them up."

"This all fits."

She asked, "Why?"

I said, "The pimps worked for Herth."

"How do you know that?"

"I know Herth."

"Oh."

"Have you been involved for ten years?"

She nodded.

"How did you—"

She shook her head. We sipped our klava for a while. Then she sighed and said, "I got involved when I was looking for something to do after my pimp was run out of the neighborhood."

I said, "Oh."

"Couldn't you tell I used to be a whore?" She was looking hard at me, and trying to make her voice sound tough and streetwise.

I shook my head and answered the thought behind the words. "It's different among Dragaerans. Prostitution isn't thought of as something to be ashamed of."

She stared at me, but I couldn't tell if she was showing disbelief or contempt. I realized that if I kept this up, I'd start to question the Dragaeran attitude too, and I didn't need any more things to question.

I cleared my throat. "When did the pimps leave?"

"We've been chasing them out gradually over the last few years. We haven't seen any around this neighborhood for months."

"Ah ha."

"You said that already."

"Things are starting to make sense."

"You think that was why Franz was murdered?"

"All the pimps gave some portion of their income to

Herth. That's how these things work."

"I see."

"Was Franz involved in breaking up the gangs?"

"He was involved in everything."

"Was he *especially* involved in that?"

"He was involved in everything."

"I see."

I drank some more klava. Now I could hold the glass, but the klava was cold. Stupid Easterners. The waiter came over, replaced the glass, filled it.

I said, "Herth is going to try to put the pimps back in business."

"You think so?"

"Yes. He'll think that he's warned you now, so you should know better."

"We'll drive them out again. They are agents of repression."

"Agents of repression?"

"Yes."

"Okay. If you drive them out again, he'll get even nastier."

I saw something flicker behind her eyes, but her voice didn't change. "We'll fight him," she said. I guess she saw some look on my face at that, because she started looking angry again. "Do you think we don't know how to fight? What do you think was involved in breaking up the gangs in the first place? Polite conversation? Do you think they just let us? Those at the top had power and lived well. They didn't just take it, you know. We can fight. We win when we fight. As Kelly says, that's because all the real fighters are on our side."

That sounded like Kelly. I was quiet for a while, then, "I don't suppose you people would consider leaving the pimps alone."

"What do you think?"

"Yeah. What happened to the tags?"

"The what?"

"The girls who worked for the pimps."

"I don't know. I joined the movement, but that was a long time ago when things were just starting. I don't know about the rest of them.''

"Don't they have a right to live, too?"

"We all have a right to live. We have a right to live without having to sell our bodies.''

I looked at her. When I'd spoken to Paresh, I had somehow gotten past his rote answers to the person underneath. With Sheryl, I couldn't. It was frustrating.

I said, "Okay. I've found out what I wanted to, and you have some information to take back to Kelly."

She nodded. "Thanks for the klava," she said.

I paid for it and we walked back out to the corner. Paresh was there, arguing loudly with a short male Easterner about something incomprehensible. Loiosh flew back to my shoulder.

"Learn anything, boss?"

"Yeah. You?"

"Nothing I wanted to know."

Paresh nodded to me. I nodded back. Sheryl smiled at me then took up a stance on the corner. I could almost see her planting her feet.

Just to be flashy, I teleported back to my office. What's a little nausea compared to flash? Heh. Vlad the Sorcerer.

I wandered around outside of the office until my stomach settled down, then went in. As I went down the hall toward the stairs, I heard Sticks talking in one of the sitting rooms. I stuck my head in. He was seated on a couch next to Chimov, a rather young guy who I'd recruited during a Jhereg war some time before. Chimov was holding one of Sticks's clubs. It was about two feet long and had a uniform diameter of maybe an inch. Sticks was holding another one, saying, "These are hickory. Oak is fine, too. It's just what you're used to, really."

"Okay," said Chimov, "but I don't see how it's any different from a lepip."

"If you hold that way, it isn't. Look. See? Hold it here, about a third of the way from the back. It's different with different clubs, depending on length and weight, but you want to get the balance right. Here. Your thumb and forefinger act like a hinge, and if you catch the guy in the stomach, or somewhere soft, you use the heel of your hand to bounce it off. This way." He demonstrated, bouncing the club off thin air, as far as I could tell.

Chimov shook his head. "Bounce? Why are you bouncing it, anyway? Can't you get more power into it holding it all the way back?"

"Sure. And if I'm trying to break a guy's knees, or his head, that's what I do. But most of the time I'm just trying to get a message across. So I bounce this off his head ten or twelve times, then mess up his face a little and tap his ribs once or twice, and he understands things that, maybe, he didn't understand before. The idea isn't to prove how tough you are, the idea is to convince him that he wants to do what you're being paid to make him do."

Chimov tried a few swings.

"Not like that," said Sticks. "Use your fingers and your wrist. If you go flailing around like that you'll just wear yourself out. There's no future in it. Here, watch. . . ."

I left them to their conversation. I knew that kind of conversation because I'd had plenty of them myself. Now it was starting to bother me.

Maybe what everyone had been saying to me was starting to affect my thinking. Worse, maybe they were right.

6 —

. . .& dirt from knees.

I nodded to Melestav as I walked past him, and plopped into my chair. Someday I'll have to describe how you go about plopping into a chair while wearing a rapier at your hip. It takes practice.

All right, Vlad. You've just made a hash of things, going in and killing that bastard, getting Herth on your tail when you didn't need to. That's done. Let's not make it worse. This is a problem just like any other problem. Find a bite-size piece of it and solve that, then go on to the next one.

I closed my eyes and took two deep breaths.

"Boss," said Melestav. "Your wife's here."

I opened my eyes. "Send her in." Cawti entered the room like an angry dzur, and looked at me as if I were the cause of her anger. Rocza was on her shoulder. Cawti shut the door behind her and sat down across from me; we looked at each other for a while. She said, "I spoke with Sheryl."

"Yeah."

"Well?"

"I'm glad to see you, too, Cawti. How's your day been?"

"Stop it, Vlad."

73

Loiosh shifted uncomfortably. I decided he didn't really have to hear this, so I got up, opened the window and let him and Rocza out. *"In a while, chum."*

"Yeah, boss." I left the window open and faced Cawti again.

"Well?" she said again.

I sat down and leaned back. "You're angry," I said.

"My, but you're perceptive."

"Don't get sarcastic with me, Cawti, I'm not in the mood for it."

"I don't really care what you're in the mood for. I want to know why you felt the need to interrogate Sheryl."

"I'm still trying to learn exactly what happened to Franz and why it happened. Talking to Sheryl was part of that."

"Why?"

"Why am I trying to find out about Franz?" I paused and considered telling her that I wanted to save her life, but decided that would be both unfair and ineffective. I said, "Partly because I said I would, I guess."

"According to her you spent the entire time mocking everything we believe in."

"According to her, perhaps I did."

"Why was it necessary?"

I shook my head.

"What," she said, biting out each word, "is that gesture supposed to mean?"

"It indicates the negative."

"I want to know what you're doing."

I stood up and took half a step toward her then sat down again. My hands opened and closed. "No," I said. "I won't tell you what I'm doing."

"You won't."

"That is correct. You saw no need to tell me when you got involved with these people, and you didn't see any need to tell me what you were doing yesterday; I see no need to give you an account of my actions."

"You seem to be doing everything you can to hurt our movement. If that isn't the case, you should—"

"No. Everything I could do to hurt your movement would be a lot simpler and be over much more quickly and leave no room for doubt. I am doing something else. You aren't with me on it because you've said you weren't. I've been trying to investigate Franz's killing on my own, and you've done everything to keep me out of it except put a knife in me, and maybe that's next. You have no right to do that and then try to interrogate me like the Imperial Prosecutor. I won't put up with it."

She glared. "That's quite a speech. It's quite a lot of crap."

"Cawti, I've made my position clear. I need not, and will not, put up with any more of this."

"If you're going to stick your nose into—"

"Get out of my office."

Her eyes widened. Then narrowed. Her nostrils flared. She stood motionless for a moment, then turned and walked out of my office. She didn't slam the door.

I sat there, trembling, until Loiosh came back. Rocza wasn't with him. I decided Rocza must be with Cawti. I was glad because I knew Cawti would need someone.

After letting Loiosh in, I walked out of the office and let my feet carry me where they would, as long as it wasn't to the Easterners' section. I felt a ridiculous urge to find the oracle I'd spoken to a couple of weeks before and kill him; even now I can't think why I wanted to do that. I actually had to talk myself out of it.

I didn't notice where I was going. I paid no attention to direction, or people around me, or anything else. A couple of Jhereg toughs saw me, took two steps toward me, then went away again. It was only much later that I realized that they had been two enforcers for an old enemy, and probably felt they had something to settle with me. I guess they changed their minds. By then Spellbreaker was in my left hand and I was swinging it as I walked, sometimes smacking it at buildings and watching parts of the walls crumble away, or just flailing wildly, hoping someone would get close enough. I don't know how much time went by, and I've never asked Loiosh, but I think I walked for over an hour.

Think about that for a minute. You've just made an enemy who has the resources to keep a tail on you wherever you go, and you've made him mad enough to kill you. So what do you do? Walk around without any protection for an hour making as big a spectacle of yourself as you can.

This is not what I call intelligent.

One cry of, "Boss!" was all Loiosh had time for. As far as I was concerned, it was like waking up from sleep to find yourself surrounded by hostile faces. Several of them. I saw at least one wizard's staff. A voice came from somewhere inside of me. It sounded absurdly calm, and it said, "You're dead now, Vlad." I don't know what that triggered, but it enabled me to think clearly. It was as if I had only an instant to do something, but the instant stretched out forever. Options came and went. Spellbreaker could probably break the teleport block they must have put around me, but there was no way I could teleport out before they had me. I might be able to take a few of them with me, which is a good thing for a Dzur hero to do if he wants to be remembered, but it felt quite futile just then. On the other hand, you don't send a group of eight or nine if you want to kill someone; maybe they had something else in mind. No way to guess what, though. I put all of the force of command I could muster into a psionic message: "Loiosh. Go away."

I felt him leave my shoulder and was ridiculously pleased. Something tingled in the back of my neck. I felt the ground against my cheek.

The first thing I heard, just before I opened my eyes, was, "You will note that you are still alive."

Then I did open them and found that I was looking at Bajinok. Before becoming aware of anything else, I remarked to myself what a perfect thing that had been for him to say. The timing, I guess, is what really got to me. I mean, just as I was becoming conscious, before I even noticed the chains holding me onto the hard iron chair or the feeling of being caught in a net of sorcery. Before, in fact, I noticed that I was naked. The chair was cold.

I looked back at him, feeling the need to say something, but not able to come up with anything. He waited, though. Just naturally polite, I guess. The room was well lighted and not too small—about twelve paces on the sides I could see (I didn't turn around). There were five enforcer types behind Bajinok, and from the way they stared at me, their hands on various pieces of hardware, they took me seriously. I felt flattered. In a corner of the room were my clothing and assorted junk. I said, "As long as you have all of my clothes in a pile, could you be a pal and have them cleaned? I'll repay you, of course."

He smiled and nodded. We were both going to be cool professionals about this. Oh, goody. I stared at him. I became aware that I wanted, almost desperately, to break the chains that were around my arms and legs and get up and kill him. Strangle him. Visions filled my brain of the enforcers battering me with their swords and spells which bounced off me or fell harmless as I squeezed the life out of him. I fought to keep this wish off my face and out of my actions. I wished Loiosh were there with me while I was glad he wasn't. I have strong opinions about ambivalence.

He pulled up a chair and sat facing me, crossed his legs, leaned back. He could have chosen to be in that position when I regained consciousness, but I guess he liked dramatic gestures as much as I do. "You are alive," he said, "because we need some answers from you."

"Ask away," I said. "I'm feeling awfully cooperative."

He nodded. "If I told you that we'll let you live if you give us the answers, you wouldn't believe me. Besides, I don't like to lie. So instead I will tell you, quite truthfully, that if you don't give us the answers, you will very badly want to die. Do you understand this?"

I nodded because my mouth was suddenly very dry. I

felt queasy. I was aware of all sorts of spells in the
room; probably spells that would prevent any sorcery I
might try. I still had my link to the Orb, of course
(which told me I'd only been unconscious for ten
minutes or so), but I doubted I could do anything with
it. Still. . . .

He said, "What is your connection to this group of
Easterners?"

I blinked. He didn't know? Maybe I could use that.
Perhaps if I stalled, I could try witchcraft. I'd used it
before in situations where I shouldn't have been able to.
I said, "Well, they're Easterners, and I'm an Easterner,
so we just sort of naturally—" Then I screamed. I can't,
now, recall what hurt. I think everything. I have no
memory of some particular part of me hurting, but I
knew that he was right; this would do it. I wanted to die.
It lasted for such a brief time that it was over before I
screamed, but I knew I couldn't take more of it, whatever it was. I was drenched with sweat, and my head
drooped and I heard myself making small whimpering
sounds like a puppy.

No one said anything. After a long time I looked up. I
felt like I had aged twenty years. Bajinok had no expression on his face. He said, "What is your connection to
the group of Easterners?"

I said, "My wife is one of them."

He nodded. So. He had known. He was going to play
that kind of game with me—asking some questions he
knew the answers to and some that he didn't. Wonderful. But that was all right, because I knew I wasn't going
to lie any more.

"Why is she with them?"

"I think she believes in what they're doing."

"What about you?"

I paused, my heart pounding with fear, but I had to
ask. "I . . . don't understand your question."

"What are you doing with those Easterners?"

A sense of relief flooded me. Yes. I could answer
that. "Cawti. I don't want her killed. Like Franz was
killed."

"What makes you think she will be?"

"I'm not sure. I don't yet—that is, I don't know why Franz was killed."

"Do you have any theories?"

I paused again, trying to understand the question, and I guess I waited too long because they hit me with it. Longer this time. Eternity. Maybe two seconds. Dear Verra, *please* let me die.

When it stopped, I couldn't speak for a moment, but I knew I had to had to had to or they'd do it again again again, so, "I'm trying. I—." I had to swallow and was afraid to, but I did, and shuddered with relief when it didn't happen. I tried to speak again. "Water," I said. A glass was tipped into my mouth. I swallowed some and spilled more down my chest. Then I spoke quickly so they wouldn't think I was trying to stall. "They were cutting into your—Herth's—business. I'm guessing it was a warning."

"Do they think so?"

"I don't know. Kelly—their leader—is smart. Also I told one of them I thought so."

"If it is a warning, will they heed it?"

"I don't think so."

"How many of them are there?"

"I've only seen about half a dozen, but I've been told that—"

I was staring right at the door when it burst open and several shiny things came flying through it past Bajinok and past my head. Their were grunts from behind me. Someone had probed the room and found the position of everyone in it. Good work. Probably Kragar.

Bajinok was fast. He didn't waste any time with me, or with the intruders, he just stepped over to one of the sorcerers and they began a teleport. Sticks, who was standing in the doorway, didn't spare more than a glance at him, before moving into the room. Something else shiny flashed by me and I heard another grunt behind my right shoulder, then noticed that Kragar was also in the doorway, throwing knives. Loiosh flew into the room then, and Glowbug was right behind him.

Glowbug's eyes were shining like the lamps at the Dragon Gate of the Imperial Palace. The thought, "You're being rescued," flashed into my head, but I couldn't drum up more than a passing interest in whether the attempt would be successful.

Watching Sticks was interesting, though. He was dealing with four of them at once. He had a club in each hand and a look of concentration on his face. The clubs became a blur, but never invisible. He was very graceful. He would bounce a club off a head, then hit a side while the other club crossed over to the top of the first head, and like that. When they tried to hit him he would work the attack into his actions as if he'd planned it all along. He started moving faster, and soon their weapons flew from their hands and they started to stumble. Then Sticks, as if culminating a dance, finished them. One at a time, both clubs to the top of the head, not quite at the same time. Ker-thump. Ker-thump. Ker-thump. Ker-thump. The first hit the ground as he nailed the third. The second hit the ground as he got the fourth. As the third fell, Sticks stepped back and looked around, and as the last one fell he put his clubs away.

Glowbug's voice came from over my shoulder. "Got 'em all, Kragar."

"Good." His voice came from right next to me, and I saw that he was working on the chains.

"You all right, boss?"

The chains fell off my arms, and I felt the ones around my legs being worked on. A lady in grey and black came into the room. Kragar said, "We'll be ready in a moment, milady." I thought, Left Hand. Sorceress. Hired to teleport us home.

"Boss?"

The chains were gone from my legs now. "Vlad?" said Kragar. "Can you stand up?"

It would be nice to collapse into bed, I decided. I noticed Glowbug collecting my clothing.

"Boss? Say something."

Sticks looked at me, then looked away. I think I saw him mouthing an obscenity.

"Damn it, boss! What's wrong?"

"All right," said Kragar. "Glowbug, help me get him standing. Gather round." I felt Loiosh clutching my shoulder. I was dragged to my feet. "Go," said Kragar.

"Boss? Can't you—"

A twist in my gut, a massive disorientation and head-spinning, and the world went around and around inside of my skull.

"—answer?"

I threw up on the ground outside of my home. They held me, and Sticks, now holding the bundle of my belongings, stood close by. "Get him inside," said Kragar. They tried to help me walk but I collapsed and almost fell.

"Boss?"

They tried again with no better results. Kragar said, "We'll never get him up the stairs this way."

"I'll dump these things inside the house, and—no, wait." Sticks vanished from sight for a moment and I heard him speaking to someone in low tones. I heard the words, "drunk" and "brothel," and what seemed to be a child's voice answering him. Then he came back without the bundle and took my legs and they carried me into the house.

Sticks dropped my legs at the top of the stairs and clapped. I heard a child say, "I'll leave these here." There was a rustling sound, and the child said, "No, that's all right," and there were soft footsteps descending. After waiting for someone to answer the clap, Sticks opened the door and I was dragged inside.

"Now what?" said Glowbug.

I could hear barely concealed distaste in Kragar's voice as he said, "We need to get him cleaned up, I think, and—Cawti!"

"Loiosh told me to come home right away. What —Vlad?"

"He needs to be cleaned up and put to bed, I think."

"Are you all right, Vlad?"

Loiosh flew off my shoulder. Probably to Cawti, but I was staring in the other direction just then so I couldn't tell. Cawti was silent for a moment, then she said, "Put him in the bath. Through here." It sounded as if she was having trouble keeping her voice steady.

After a while there was hot water on me, and Cawti's hands were gentle. I learned that I'd soiled myself somewhere in there, as well as throwing up all over my chest and stomach. Kragar came into the room and he and Cawti got me standing and dried me off, then got me into the bed and left me there. Loiosh, silent now, sat next to me, his head on my cheek. Rocza made scratching sounds on the bedpost to my left.

From the next room, I could hear Cawti saying, "Thank you, Kragar."

Kragar said, "Thank Loiosh." Then their voices dropped and I could only hear mutterings for a while.

Later, the door to the flat closed and I heard Cawti make her way into the bathroom, and the sound of the pump. After a while she came back into the bedroom and put a damp cloth over my forehead. She put Spellbreaker around my left wrist and covered me with blankets. I settled back into the bedding and waited to die.

It was funny. I'd always wondered what my last thoughts would be, if I had time to think them. It turned out that my last thoughts were of how I was thinking my last thoughts. That was funny. I chuckled somewhere, deep down inside of me where I can't be hurt. If Aliera was right about reincarnation, perhaps my next life would be better. No. I *knew* Aliera was right. My next life probably wouldn't be any better than this one. Well, I don't know. Maybe you learn something each life. What had I learned in this lifetime? That it's always the good guys against the bad guys, and you can never tell who the good guys are, so you settle for killing the bad guys. We're all bad guys. No. Loiosh isn't a bad guy. Cawti isn't—well—oh, what's the use? I should just—

—I realized with some surprise that I was still alive. It occurred to me then that I might *not* die. I felt my heart speed up. Was it possible? A certain sense of what I could only call reality began to seep in then, and I knew

I was going to live. I still couldn't accept it emotionally—I didn't really believe it—but I somehow knew it. I reached for my right sleeve dagger but it was gone. Then I remembered that I was naked. I lifted my head and saw the bundle of my clothing and weapons, with the rapier jutting out, over in the corner, and I knew I couldn't reach it. I felt Spellbreaker around my left wrist. Would that do? How? I could hardly strangle myself. Maybe I could bash myself over the head.

I worked my left arm free and stared at the thin gold chain. When I first found it, Sethra Lavode had suggested I find a name for it. She was evasive when I asked why. Now I looked at it closely, wrapped tightly about my wrist, clinging, but never squeezing. I let my arm fall off the side of the bed and it uncoiled and fell into my hand. I lifted it, and it worked itself into a pose, hanging in midair like a coiled yendi. As I moved my hand, the rest of it didn't move, as if the other end was fixed in space, twelve inches above me.

What are you? I asked it. *You have saved my life more than once, but I don't really know what you are. Are you a weapon? Can you kill me now?*

It coiled and uncoiled then, as if it were considering the matter. I had never seen it do that before. The trick of hanging in midair it had been doing when I had first found it, but that had been under Dzur Mountain, where strange things are normal. Or was it in the Paths of the Dead? I couldn't remember any more. Did it mean to take me back there now? Easterners aren't allowed into the Paths of the Dead, but was I really an Easterner? What *was* an Easterner, really? Were they different from Dragaerans? Who cared? That was easy, Easterners cared and Dragaerans cared. Who *didn't* care? Kelly didn't care. Did the Lords of Judgment care?

Spellbreaker formed shapes in the air before me, twisting and coiling like a dancer. I barely noticed when Loiosh flew out of the room. It was still dancing for me a few minutes later when Cawti returned, holding a steaming cup of tea.

"Drink this, Vlad," she said, her voice trembling. Spellbreaker dipped low, then climbed high. I wondered what would happen if I let go of the end I was holding, but didn't want to take the chance that it would stop. I felt a cup pressed against my lip and hot tea dribbled into my mouth and onto my chest. I swallowed by reflex and noticed an odd taste. It occurred to me that perhaps Cawti was poisoning me. When the cup came again, I drank greedily, still watching Spellbreaker's dance.

When the cup was empty, I lay back, waiting for oblivion. There was some part of me that was mildly surprised when it came.

7 -

1 pr black riding boots:
remove reddish stain on toe of rt boot. . .

I don't remember actually waking up. I stared at the
ceiling for a long time without focusing on it. Aware-
ness of sensations increased slowly—the smooth linen of
finely woven sheets, the scent of Cawti's hair next to my
face, her warm, dry hand in mine. With my other hand I
touched myself, face and body, and I blinked. Loiosh's
tail was draped across my neck—feather-light and scaly.

"Boss?" Tentative.

"Yes, Loiosh. I'm here."

He rested his head against my cheek. I smelled Adrilankha's morning in the breeze through the window. I
licked my lips, squeezed my eyes tightly shut, and
opened them. Memory returned, piercing as a needle. I
winced, then trembled. After a moment I turned toward
Cawti. She was awake and looking at me. Her eyes were
red. I said, "Some of us will do anything for sym-
pathy." My voice cracked as I said it. She squeezed my
hand.

After a moment, she chuckled softly. "I'm trying to
find a way to say, 'Are you all right?' that doesn't
sound like you ought to be put away somewhere." I
squeezed her hand. Loiosh stirred and flapped around

the room once. Rocza stirred from somewhere and hissed.

"If you mean am I about to kill myself, the answer is no." Then I said, "You didn't sleep, did you?" She made a gesture that I took as, "No, I didn't." I said, "Maybe you should." She looked at me with swimming red eyes. I said, "You know, this doesn't really solve anything."

"I know," she said, and this time it was her voice that broke. "Do you want to talk about it?"

"About—what happened yesterday? No. It's too close. What did you give me? It *was* a poison, wasn't it?"

"In the tea? Yes. Tsiolin, but just a mild dose so you'd sleep."

I nodded. She moved over next to me and I held her. I stared at the ceiling a while longer. It was made of beaded ceiling board, and Cawti had painted it a very pale green. "Green?" I had said at the time. "It represents growth and fertility," she had explained. "Ah ha," I had said and we went on to other things. Now it just looked green. But she was holding me. Make of this what you will.

I got up and took care of morning things. When I looked back in, Cawti was sleeping. I went out with Loiosh and sat in Kigg's for a while and drank klava. I was very careful to watch all around as I left home. I've never been attacked when I was ready for it; it's always come unexpectedly. That's odd only because of the amount of time I seem to spend expecting to be attacked. I wondered what it would be like not to have to worry about that. If these Easterners had their way, and their daydreams turned out real, that might happen. But it wouldn't matter to me, anyway. I couldn't remember a time when I wasn't careful to watch around me as much as possible. Even when I was young there were too many kids who didn't like Easterners. I was stuck as I was, whatever happened. But still—

"I think you have too much on your mind, boss."

I nodded. *"All right, chum. Tell me what to ignore."*

"Heh."

"Right."

"About these Easterners—Kelly's group. . . ."

"Yeah?"

"What if you didn't have to worry about Cawti's life, or about Herth, or any of it. How would you feel about them?"

"How can I know that?"

"How would you feel about Cawti being one of them?"

Now that was a good question. I chewed it over. "I guess I just don't think much of a group that's so wrapped up in its ideals that it doesn't care about people."

"But about Cawti—"

"Yeah. I don't know, Loiosh. There was never really the chance to find out what's involved. How much time will it take? Am I going to see her at all? Is she going to want to give them money? How much? There are too many things I don't know. She ought to have told me about it."

I drank some more klava and thought about things. I was very careful walking out of the place.

When I got into the office I didn't stop long enough to say hello to Kragar and Melestav; I went straight into the basement. Next to the lab is a large, empty room with many lanterns. I lit them. I drew my rapier, saluted my shadow, and attacked it.

Parry head. What had happened to me last night?

Step in, step out. It was worse than being told I was a reincarnated Dragaeran. Or different, at least.

Step in, cut flank, step out. Maybe I should just forget that I'd tried to kill myself. Except that I might try again, and maybe I'd succeed. But then, maybe it would have been best if I had.

Step in, cut cheek, cut neck, step out. That was nonsense. On the other hand, there was no denying that I had actually wanted to kill myself last night; had tried to do so. It was hard to believe.

Parry flank, parry head, step in, cut leg, thrust chest.
The pain, though—that incredible pain. But it was over.
I was going to have to get to Herth before he got to me,
and it might not change how Cawti felt toward me
anyway, and I wouldn't even get paid for it. But no matter; I would have to make sure he couldn't do that to me
again. Ever.

Step back, parry a thrust, disengage, stop-cut, step in,
cut neck. I'm not the suicidal type. There are many
assassins who don't care if they live or die, but I've
never been one. Or I never was one before. Forget it. I
could spend the rest of my life trying to decide what it
meant that I'd wanted to end it. There were things that I
had to do and this was getting nowhere. I was going to
have to kill Herth, and that was that.

Salute. I just wished I didn't have to.

I also wished I'd installed a bath down here.

"Kragar."

"Yeah?"

"I'm done mucking about."

"Good. It's about time."

"Shut up. I want full details on Herth. I mean,
everything. I want to know his mistress's favorite color
and how often she washes her hair. I want to how much
pepper he puts in his soup. I want to know how often he
takes a—"

"Right, boss. I'll get on it."

"*Can you get him before anything happens to
Cawti?*"

"*I don't know. I don't know for sure that anything
will happen to Cawti. But we can't take chances. I'll
have to—*" I paused as a thought hit me. I threw it away
and it came back. There was one thing I could do that
might help.

"*She isn't going to like it if she finds out, boss.*"

"*By Verra's fingers, Loiosh! She hasn't liked
anything I've done since this mess started. So what? Do
you have any other ideas?*"

"*I guess not.*"

"Neither do I. I should have done this days ago. I haven't been thinking. Is Rocza with her now?"

He paused. *"Yes."*

"Then let's go."

"What about protection for you?"

I felt suddenly queasy as I remembered the day before. *"I'm not going to be charging around like a blind man this time."*

"Aren't you?"

That sounded rhetorical so I didn't answer.

I teleported directly from my office, just in case someone was waiting outside. The Easterners' section was starting to look more and more familiar as I spent more and more time there. I had mixed feelings about this.

I asked, *"Is she moving?"*

"She was, boss. She stopped a while ago."

"How far are we?"

"I could fly there in five minutes."

"Great. How far are we?"

"Half an hour."

Streets curved and twisted like Verra's sense of humor, and it was, in fact, a good half-hour before we found ourselves near a large park. A crowded park. There were thousands there, mostly human. I gawked. The last time I had seen that many people gathered in one place there was a battle being fought. I hadn't liked it.

I took a deep breath and began to make my way into and through the crowd, Loiosh steering. (*"This way. Okay, now back to the right. Over there, somewhere."*) Loiosh was being careful not to let Rocza know he was in the area. He could have been unhappy about it, but I guess he chose to look at it as a game. I was being careful not to let Cawti know I was in the area, and there was nothing gamelike about it.

I spotted her, standing on a platform that seemed to be the center of the crowd's attention. She was scanning the crowd, although most people looking at her wouldn't have known it. At first I thought she was look-

ing for me, but then I understood and chuckled. Kelly
was standing at the front of the platform, declaiming in
a thundering voice about "their" fear of "us," and
Cawti was acting as his bodyguard. Great. I moved up
toward the platform, shaking my head. I wanted to act
as *her* bodyguard, without her seeing me. She was looking for someone trying to sneak up to the platform—in
other words, she was looking for someone doing just
what I was trying to do.

When I realized that, I stopped where I was—about
forty feet away—and watched. I really can't tell you
what the speech was about; I wasn't listening. He didn't
turn the crowd into a raging mob, but they seemed interested, and there were occasional cheers. I felt lost. I'd
never before been in a large group of people while trying
to decide if one member of the group was going to kill
another member. I assume there are ways of doing it,
but I don't know them. I checked back on the platform
from time to time, but nothing was happening. I occasionally caught phrases from Kelly's speech, things like,
"historical necessity," and "we aren't going to them on
our knees." In addition to Kelly, Gregory was up there,
and Natalia, and several Easterners and a few Teckla I
didn't recognize. They also seemed to be interested in
whatever Kelly was talking about.

Eventually the gathering broke up with much cheer-
ing. I tried to stay as close behind Cawti as I could
without being spotted. It wasn't very close. Groups
formed, one around each of those who had been on the
platform, except for Cawti. She was hanging around
Kelly. As things thinned out I kept expecting to see
someone else who, like me, was just sort of lagging
behind, but I didn't.

After half an hour, Kelly, Gregory and Natalia left
the area. Things were pretty quiet by then. I followed
them. They returned to Kelly's house and disappeared
inside. I waited. The weather was good, for which I was
grateful; I hate standing around waiting in the cold and
rain.

The trouble was, it left me with too much time to

think, and I had too much to think about.

I had actually tried to kill myself. Why? That had been the first time I'd been tortured, certainly, but I'd had information beaten out of me before; was it really all that different? I thought of the pain and heard myself screaming and a shudder ran through my body.

Other times, when I'd been forced to give up information, I had been in control. I had been able to play with them—giving them this or that tidbit and holding back what I could. This time I had just spilled my guts. Okay, but that still didn't account for it. I'm just not the suicidal type. Am I? Verra, what's wrong with me?

After a while I said, *"Loiosh, keep watching the house. I'm going to visit Noish-pa."*

"No, boss. Not without me."

"What? Why not?"

"Herth is still looking for you."

"Oh. Yeah."

Cawti came out of the house after a few hours. It was getting on toward evening. She headed toward home. I followed. A few times Rocza, on her shoulder, began looking around nervously and Loiosh suggested we drop back for a while, so we did. That was pretty much the excitement. I wandered around for an hour or so then went home myself. Cawti and I didn't say a lot, but I caught her looking at me a few times with a worried expression on her face.

You can repeat a lot of that for the next day. She left the house and I followed her while she stood around selling tabloids (a new one, I saw; the banner said something about landlords) and talking to strangers. I watched the strangers closely, especially the occasional Dragaeran. I checked with Kragar to see how he was doing, and he said he was working on it. I left him alone after that. I had only bothered him at all because of a growing sense of frustration.

Frustration? Sure. I was following Cawti around desperately trying to keep her alive and knowing that it was pointless. I couldn't be sure they were about to kill one of the Easterners, and there was no reason to think it

would be Cawti and, frankly, there wasn't much I could
do anyway. Assassins work by surprise. But if the assassin can surprise the target, chances are he can also
surprise one bodyguard who is twenty or thirty feet
away. Trying to protect Cawti was almost an exercise in
futility. But then, there wasn't anything else I could do
except think, and I was tired of thinking.

"Boss."

I glanced in the direction that had Loiosh's attention.
It was the corner of a large, brown building—the kind
that has flats for several families. *"What is it?"*

*"I saw someone there, tall enough to be a Dra-
gaeran."*

I watched for a while but there was no further movement. Cawti still stood next to a vegetable stall, along
with Sheryl, exchanging comments with the vendor from
time to time. For half an hour I alternated between
watching Cawti and watching the corner, then I gave up
and went back to watching my wife while Loiosh kept
an eye on the spot where he'd seen someone. Eventually
Cawti and Sheryl left and walked back to the building I
thought of as their headquarters, though Cawti referred
to it only as Kelly's place. I tried to see if they were
being followed, but I couldn't be certain.

Cawti went inside and Sheryl kept going. I stationed
myself out of sight down the street where I could watch
the door. I was getting to know that door better than I'd
ever wanted to know a door. I was glad, at least, that
Cawti couldn't teleport.

It was getting on toward evening when a Dragaeran in
Jhereg colors walked boldly up to the door and inside. I
checked my weapons and started after him quickly, but
he was out again before I was halfway across the street.
I turned the other way and seemed uninterested and he
didn't notice me. When I looked back he was walking
hurriedly away. I thought about following him, but the
most I could do was confirm that Herth had sent him.
So what?

He was, I decided, probably a messenger. Or he could

have been a sorcerer and he'd just killed everyone in the house. Or—at that moment Cawti, Paresh and Natalia left as if they were in a hurry. I followed. They headed northeast, which is toward the center of the city. (The Easterners' section is South Adrilankha, which is mostly west of central Adrilankha. Make sense of that if you care to.)

Before crossing the unmarked border into Dragaeran terrain (a street called Carpenter), they turned and followed a couple of side streets. Eventually they stopped and gathered around something on the ground. Cawti knelt down while the others stood over. Paresh began looking around. I walked toward them and he saw me. He straightened quickly and his hand went up as if he were about to do something sorcerous and Spellbreaker came into my hand. But he did nothing, and presently I was close enough to be recognized in the fading orange-red light, as well as to see that Cawti was kneeling next to a body. She looked up.

Paresh was tense, the muscles on his neck standing out. Natalia seemed only mildly interested and a bit fatalistic. Cawti stared at me hard.

Paresh said, "What have you to do with this?"

"Nothing," I said, figuring I'd allow him exactly one such question. He nodded rather than pushing it, which half disappointed me.

Cawti said, "What are you doing here, Vlad?"

Instead of answering, I approached the body. I looked, then looked away, then looked again, longer. It had once been Sheryl. She had been beaten to death. She was not revivifiable. Each leg was broken at the knee, above it, and below. Each arm was broken at the elbow. The bruises on each side of her face—what was left of it—matched. The top of her head had been staved in. And so on. It was my professional judgment that it had been done over the course of several hours. And if you can't make professional judgments, what's the point of being a professional? I looked away again.

"What are you doing here, Vlad?" asked Cawti.

"I was following you."

She looked at me, then nodded, as if to herself. "Did you see anything?"

"Loiosh maybe caught a glimpse of someone watching while you were at the market, but then you went into Kelly's place and I just watched the door."

"You didn't see fit to tell anyone?"

I blinked. Tell someone? One of them? Well, I suppose that made sense. "It didn't occur to me."

She stared, then turned her back. Paresh was almost glaring at me. Natalia was looking away, but when I looked closer, I could see that she was almost trembling with anger. Cawti's hands were closed into fists, and she was tightening and loosening them rhythmically. I felt myself start to get angry, too. They didn't want me around at all; they certainly hadn't asked me to watch Sheryl. Now they were all at the boiling point because I hadn't. It was enough to—

"They aren't mad at you, boss."

"Eh?"

"They're mad at Herth for doing it, and maybe at themselves for having allowed him to."

"How could they have prevented it?"

"Don't ask me."

I turned to Paresh, who was closest. "How could you have prevented it?"

He just shook his head. Natalia answered, though, in a strained voice, as if she could barely speak. "We could have built the movement faster and stronger, so they wouldn't have dared to do this. They should be scared of us by now."

This wasn't the time to explain what I thought of that. Instead, I helped them carry Sheryl's body back to Kelly's place. We didn't get more than a few glances as we made our way through the darkening streets. I suppose that says something. The three of them acted as if I should feel honored that they were allowing me to help. I didn't comment on that, either. We left the body in the hallway while they went in and I left without saying anything.

On the way over to Noish-pa's I was taken with the irrational fear that I would find him murdered. I'll save you the suspense and tell you that he was fine, but it's interesting that I felt that way.

As I walked past the chimes he called out, "Who is there?"

"Vlad," I said.

We hugged and I sat down next to Ambrus. Noish-pa puttered around putting on tea and talking about the new spice dealer he'd found who still soaked absinthe in mint-water for a fortnight, the way it was supposed to be done. (A fortnight, if you're interested, is one day less than three weeks. If you think that's a peculiar period of time for which to have a special term, I can't blame you.)

When the tea was done and appreciated and I had made a respectful hello to Ambrus while Noish-pa did the same to Loiosh, he said, "What troubles you, Vladimir?"

"Everything, Noish-pa."

He looked at me closely. "You haven't been sleeping well."

"No."

"For our family, that is a bad sign."

"Yes."

"What has happened?"

"Do you remember that fellow, Franz, who was killed?"

He nodded.

"Well," I said, "there's another one. I was there when they found her body just now."

He shook his head. "And Cawti is still with these people?"

I nodded. "It's more than that, Noish-pa. They're like children who've found a Morganti dagger. They don't know what they're doing. They just keep going about their business as if they could stand up to the whole Jhereg, not to mention the Empire itself. That wouldn't bother me if Cawti weren't one of them, but I just can't protect her; not forever. I was standing outside their meeting place when the messenger showed up to tell them where to find the body—or so I assume. But he could just as easily have been a sorcerer and destroyed the entire house and everyone in it. I know the guy behind it—he'd do it. They don't seem to understand that and I can't convince them."

After I'd run down, Noish-pa shifted in his chair, looking thoughtful. Then he said, "You say you know this man, who is doing these things?"

"Not well, but I know of him."

"If he can do this, why hasn't he?"

"It hasn't been worth his effort, yet. It costs money and he won't spend more than he has to."

He nodded. "I'm told they had a gathering yesterday."

"What? Oh, yeah. In a park near here."

"Yes. They had a parade, too. It went by. There were a lot of people."

"Yes." I thought back to the park. "A few thousand, anyway. But so what? What can they do?"

"Perhaps you should speak to this Kelly again, try to convince him."

I said, "Maybe."

After a while he said, "I have never seen you so unhappy, Vladimir."

I said, "It's my work, I suppose, one way or another. We play by rules, you know? If you leave us alone, we'll leave you alone. If somebody gets hurt who isn't part of the organization, it means he was sticking his nose where it didn't belong. That isn't our fault, that's just how it is. Kelly's people did that—they butted in where they shouldn't have. Only they didn't, really. They—I don't know. Damn them to Verra's dungeons, anyway. Sometimes I wish I could just complete Herth's job for him, and sometimes I'd like to—I don't know what. And you know, I can't even get a good enough feel for Herth to send him for a walk. I'm too tied up in this. I ought to hire someone to do it for me, but I just *can't*. Don't you see that? I have to—" I blinked. I'd been rambling. I'd lost Noish-pa some time before. I wondered what he thought of all that.

He looked at me with a somber expression on his face. Loiosh flew over onto my shoulder and squeezed. I drank some more tea. Noish-pa said, "And Cawti?"

"I don't know. Maybe she feels the same way, and that's why she found these people. She killed me, you know."

His eyes widened. I said, "That's how we met. She was hired to kill me and she did. I've never killed an East—a human. She has. And now she's acting as if—never mind."

He studied me, and I suppose he remembered our last conversation, because he asked, "How long have you been doing this, Vladimir? This killing of people."

He sounded genuinely interested in the answer, so I said, "Years."

He nodded. "It is perhaps time that you thought about it."

I said, "Suppose I'd joined the Phoenix Guard, if they'd have me. One way or another, that's killing people for money. Or enlisted in some Dragonlord's private army, for that matter. What's the difference?"

"Perhaps there is none. I have no answer for you, Vladimir. I only say that perhaps it is time you thought about it."

"Yeah," I said. "I'm thinking about it."

He poured more tea and I drank it and after a while I went home.

. . .& remove dust & soot from both. . .

I remember the Wall of Baritt's Tomb.

It wasn't really a tomb, you understand; there was no body inside. The Serioli go in for tombs. They build them either underground or in the middle of mountains, and they put dead people in them. It seems weird to me. The Dragaerans sometimes build monuments to dead big shots like Baritt, and when they build one they call it a tomb because it looks like what the Serioli use and because Dragaerans aren't too bright.

Baritt's Tomb was huge in every dimension, a grey slate monstrosity, with pictures and symbols carved into it. It was stuck way out in the east, high up in the Eastern Mountains near a place where Dragaerans trade with Easterners for eastern red pepper and other things. I got stuck in the middle of a battle there once. I've never forgotten how it felt. One army was made up of Easterners who died, the other was made up of Teckla who died. On the Dragaerans' side were a couple of Dragonlords who were never really in any danger. That's one memory that stays with me. No one was going to hurt Morrolan or Aliera, and they laid about themselves like pip-squeak deities. The other thing I remember was watching all of this happen and almost chewing my lip off from helplessness.

The venture wasn't useless, you understand. I mean, Morrolan got a good fight, Sethra the Younger got Kieron's greatsword while Aliera got one more her size, and I got to learn that you can never go home. But in the battle itself there was nothing I could do unless I wanted to be one of the Teckla or one of the Easterners who were falling like ash from Mount Zerika. I didn't, so I just watched.

That's what came back to me now. Every time I feel helpless, in fact, that memory returns to haunt me. Each scream from each wounded Easterner, or even Teckla, remains with me. I know that Dragons consider assassination to be less "honorable" than butchering Easterners, but I've never quite understood why. That battle showed me what futility was, though. So many deaths for such a small result.

Of course, I finally did . . . something—but that's another tale. What I remember is the helplessness.

Cawti wasn't speaking to me.

It wasn't that she refused to say anything, it was more that she didn't have anything to say. I walked around the house in bare feet all morning, swatting halfheartedly at jhereg who got in my way and staring out various windows hoping one of them would show something interesting. I threw a couple of knives at our hall target and missed. Eventually I collected Loiosh and walked over to my office, being very careful all the way.

Kragar was waiting for me. He looked unhappy. That was all right; why should he be any different?

"What is it?" I asked him.

"Herth."

"What about him?"

"He doesn't have a mistress, he doesn't eat soup, and he never takes a—"

"What do you mean? You can't find out anything about him?"

"No, I tracked him pretty well. The good news is that he isn't a sorcerer. But other than that, he's like you; he doesn't have any regular schedule. And he doesn't have an office; he works right out of his home. He never visits the same inn twice in a row, and I haven't found any pattern at all to his movements.''

I sighed. "I half expected that. Well, keep on it. Eventually something will show up. No one lives a completely random life."

He nodded and walked out.

I put my feet up on the desk, then took them down again. I got up and paced. It hit me once more that Herth was planning to send me for a walk. There was probably someone out there, right now, trying to pin down my movements so he could get me. I looked out my office window but I didn't see anyone standing in the street opposite my door holding a dagger. I sat down again. Even if I managed to get Herth first, whoever it was had still taken the money, was still committed to getting me. I shivered.

There was one thing, at least: I could relax about Cawti for a while. Herth had given them another subtle warning. He wouldn't do anything else until he saw what effect that had. This meant that I could work on keeping myself alive. How? Well, I could gain some time by killing whoever was after me, which would force Herth to go to the bother of finding another assassin.

Good idea, Vlad. Now, how you gonna do it?

I thought of a way. Loiosh didn't like it. I asked him if he had any other suggestions and he didn't. I decided to do it at once, before I could consider how stupid it was. I got up and walked out of the office without speaking to anyone.

Loiosh tried to spot him as I wandered around the neighborhood, checking on my businesses, but didn't manage. Either I wasn't being followed, or the guy was skilled. I spent the late morning and early afternoon at this. My own effort wasn't so much directed at spotting my assassin as at looking as if I felt safe. Trying to appear calm under such circumstances is not easy.

Finally, as the afternoon wore on, I headed back for the Easterners' section. There, at the same time as I had on the previous two days, I stationed myself near Kelly's headquarters and I waited. I had no more than passing interest in who went in and out of there, but I noticed that it was quite active. Cawti showed up with my friend Gregory, each of them carrying large boxes. Easterners and Teckla I didn't recognize ran in and out of the place all day. As I said, though, I didn't watch too closely. I was waiting for the assassin to make his move.

This was not the perfect place to get me, you understand; I was mostly hidden by the corner of a building and could see nearly everywhere around me. Loiosh watched over my head. But it was the only place I'd been going to at a regular time over the past few days. If I could keep this up, he'd realize that it was his best shot at me. He'd take it, and maybe I could kill him, which would give me a rest while Herth found someone else.

The unfortunate part was that I had no idea when he'd move. Staying alert for an attack for several hours is not easy, especially when what you want is to go charging out and hurt someone just for the sake of doing so.

Easterners and Teckla continued to come and go from Kelly's place. As the afternoon wore on, they would leave carrying large stacks of paper. One of them, a Teckla I didn't recognize, had a pot and brushes as well as the sheets of paper, and he started gluing them up on the walls of buildings. Passers-by stopped to read them, then went on their way.

I spent several hours there and the presumed assassin never showed. That was all right; he probably wasn't in a hurry. It was also possible he had a better idea for where to shine me. I was especially careful as I began to walk home. I arrived without incident.

Cawti still wasn't home when I dropped off to sleep.

The next day I got up without waking her. I cleaned up the place a bit, made some klava, and sat around drinking it and shadow-fencing. Loiosh was involved in some sort of deep conversation with Rocza until Cawti got up a bit later and took her out. Cawti left without saying a word. I stayed around the house until late in the afternoon, when I went back to that same spot.

The previous day I'd noticed that Kelly's people had seemed busy. Today the place was empty. There was no activity of any kind. After a while, I carefully left my little niche and looked at one of the posters they'd been gluing up the day before. It announced a rally, to be held today, and said something about ending oppression and murder.

I thought about finding the rally but decided I didn't want to deal with one of those again. I went back to my spot and waited. It was just about then that they began to show up. Kelly came back first, along with Paresh. Then several I didn't recognize, then Cawti, then more I didn't recognize. Most of them were Easterners, but there were a few Teckla.

They kept coming, too. There was a constant stream of traffic through that little place, and still more milling around outside. It made me so curious that a couple of times I caught myself paying more attention to them than to the probable assassin who was probably watching me. This would be—what?—the fourth day I'd stationed myself there. If the assassin were reckless, he'd have taken me on the third. If he were exceptionally careful, he'd wait another couple of days, or for a place more to his liking. What would I have done? Interesting question. I would either have waited for a better place, or made my move today. I almost smiled, thinking of it that way. Today is the day I would have killed myself if I'd been paid to.

I shook my head. My mind was wandering again. Loiosh took off from my shoulder, flew around a bit, then resumed his place.

"He's either not here or he's well hidden, boss."

"Yeah. What do you make of the goings-on across the street?"

"Don't know. They're stirred up like a bees' nest, though."

It didn't die down, either. As the afternoon wore on, more and more Easterners, and a few Teckla, would go into Kelly's flat for a while and come out, often carrying stacks of paper. I noticed one group of about six emerging with black headbands that they hadn't been wearing when they went in. A bit later another group went in, and they also wore the headbands when they came out. Cawti, as well as the others I knew, were popping in and out every hour or so. Once when she emerged she had on one of the headbands, too. I could only see it across her forehead because it matched her hair so well, but I thought it looked pretty good.

It was getting on toward evening when I noticed that one group loitering around the place had sticks. I looked closer and saw that one of them had a knife. I licked my lips, reminded myself to stay alert for my man, and kept watching.

I still didn't know what was going on, but I wasn't surprised, as another hour or so came and went, to see more and more groups of Easterners carrying sticks, knives, cleavers, and even an occasional sword or spear.

Something, it seemed, was Happening.

My feelings were mixed. In an odd way I was pleased. I had had no idea that these people could get together anything on the kind of scale—there were now maybe a hundred or so armed Easterners hanging around the street—that they were managing. I took a sort of vicarious pride in it. But I also knew that, if this continued, they would attract the kind of attention that could get them all hurt. My palms were sweaty, and it wasn't just from worrying about the assassin I assumed must be nearby.

In fact, I realized, I could almost relax about him. If he were the gutsy type, now would be a perfect time to get me. But if he'd been the gutsy type, he would have moved yesterday or the day before. I had the feeling he was more my kind. I wouldn't have gone near a situation like this. I like to stick to a plan, and a hundred armed, angry Easterners were unlikely to have been part of this guy's plan.

The street continued to fill up. In fact, it was becoming out and out crowded. Easterners with weapons were walking directly in front of me. It was all I could do to remain unnoticed; part of the street and not really there. I couldn't for the life of me figure out what they were doing other than milling around, but they all seemed to think it important. I considered leaving, since I was pretty certain that the presumed assassin would have left long ago.

About then the door to Kelly's place opened and Kelly came out flanked by Paresh and Cawti, with a couple of Easterners I didn't recognize in front of him. I don't know what that guy has, but I couldn't believe how quiet everything got. All of a sudden the entire street was silent. It was eerie. Everybody gathered around Kelly and waited, and they must have been practically holding their breaths to make so little noise.

He didn't get up on any kind of platform or anything, and he was pretty short, so he was completely hidden from me. I only gradually became aware that he was speaking, as if he'd started in a whisper and was talking louder and louder as he went. Since I couldn't hear him, I tried to judge the reaction he was getting. It was hard to tell, but it was quite certain that everyone was listening.

As his voice rose, I began to catch occasional phrases, then larger portions of his speech as he shouted it. "They are asking us," he declaimed, "to pay for their excesses, and we are saying we won't do it. They have forfeited any rights they may once have had to rule our destinies. We have now the right—and the obligation —to rule our own." Then his voice suddenly dropped again, but a little later it rose once more. "You, gathered here now, are only the vanguard, and this battle is only the first." And, still later, "We are not blind to their strengths, as they are blind to ours, but we're not blind to their weaknesses, either."

There was more like that, but I was too far away to get a good idea of what was going on. Still, they were waving weapons in the air, and I saw that the street was even more full than it had been when he'd started speaking. Those in back could no more hear than I could, but they pressed forward, eagerly. The atmosphere was almost carnivallike, especially far back in the crowd. They would hold up their sticks or knives or kitchen cleavers and wave them about, yelling. They would clasp each other's shoulders, or hug each other, and I saw an Easterner nearly cut the throat of a Teckla he was trying to hug.

They had no understanding of or respect for their weapons. I decided I was scared and had better leave. I stepped out of my corner and headed home. I made it with no trouble.

When Cawti arrived, close to midnight, her eyes were glowing. More than her eyes, in fact. It was as if there were a light shining inside of her head, and some of the luminescence was coming out of the pores of her skin. She had a smile on her face, and her smallest movements, as she took off her cloak and got a wine glass from the buffet, had an enthusiasm and verve that couldn't be missed. She was still wearing the black headband.

She had looked at me that way, once upon a time.

She poured herself a glass of wine and came into the living room, sat down.

"What is it?" I asked her.

"We're finally doing something," she said. "We're moving. This is the most exciting thing I can remember."

I kept my reaction off my face as best I could. "And what is this thing?"

She smiled and the light from the candles made her eyes dance. "We're shutting it down."

"Shutting what down?"

"The entire Easterners' quarter—all of South Adrilankha."

I blinked. "What do you mean, shutting it down?"

"No traffic into or out of South Adrilankha. All the merchants and peasants who pass through from the west will have to go around. There are barricades being set up all along Carpenter and Twovine. They'll be manned in the morning."

I struggled with that for a moment. Finally, "What will that do?" won out over "How are you doing it?"

She said, "Do you mean short-term, or what are we trying to achieve?"

"Both," I said. I struggled with how to put the question, then came up with, "Aren't you trying to get the peasants on your side? It sound like this will just make them mad if they have to travel all the way around South Adrilankha."

"First of all, most of them won't want to go around, so they'll sell to Easterners or go back."

"And that will get them on your side?"

She said, "They were born on our side." I had some trouble with that, but I let her continue. "It isn't as if we're trying to recruit them, or convince them to join something, or show what great people we are. We're fighting a war."

"And you don't care about civilian casualties?"

"Oh, stop it. Of course we do."

"Then why are you taking food out of the mouths of these peasants who are just trying to—"

"You're twisting things. Look, Vlad, it's time we struck back. We have to. We can't let them think they can cut us down with impunity, and the only defense we have is to bring together the masses in their own defense. And yes, some will be hurt. But the big merchants—the Orcas and the Tsalmoth and the Jhegaala—will run out of meat for their slaughterhouses. They'll be hurt more. And the nobility, who are used to eating meat once or twice every day, will be very unhappy about it after a while."

"If they're really hurt, they'll just ask the Empire to move in."

"Let them ask. And let the Empire try. We have the entire quarter, and that's only the beginning. There aren't enough Dragons in the Guard to reopen it."

"Why can't they just teleport past your barricades?"

"They can. Let them. Watch what happens when they try."

"What will happen? The Phoenix Guard are trained warriors, and one of them can—"

"Do nothing when he's outnumbered ten or twenty or thirty to one. We have all of South Adrilankha already, and that's only the beginning. We are finding support in the rest of the city and among the larger estates surrounding it. That, in fact, is what I'm going to be working on starting tomorrow. I'm going to visit some of those slaughterhouses and—"

"I see. All right, then: why?"

"Our demands to the Empress—"

"Demands? To the Empress? Are you serious?"

"Yes."

"Uh . . . all right. What are they?"

"We have asked for a full investigation into the murders of Sheryl and Franz."

I stared at her. I swallowed, then stared some more. Finally I said, "You can't mean it."

"Of course we mean it."

"You went to the Empire?"

"Yes."

"Do you mean to tell me that, not only have you gone to the Empire over a Jhereg killing, but you are now *demanding* that it be investigated?"

"That's right."

"That's crazy! Cawti, I can see Kelly or Gregory coming up with a notion like that, but you *know* how we operate."

"We?"

"Cut it out. You were in the organization for years. You know what happens when someone goes to the Empire. Herth will kill every one of you."

"Every one of us? Each of the thousands of Easterners—and Dragaerans—in South Adrilankha?"

I shook my head. She knew better. She *had* to know better. You never, never, *never* talk to the Empire. That is one of the few things that can make a Jhereg mad enough to hire someone to use a Morganti blade. Cawti *knew* that. And yet here she was, positively glowing about how they had just put all of their heads on the executioner's block.

"Cawti, don't you realize what you're doing?"

She looked at me hard. "Yes. I realize exactly what we're doing. I don't think you do. You seem to think Herth is some sort of god. He isn't. He certainly isn't strong enough to defeat an entire city."

"But—"

"And that isn't the point, anyway. We aren't counting on the Empire to give us justice. We know better, and so does everyone who lives in South Adrilankha. The thousands who are following us in this aren't doing it because they love us, but because of their *need*. There will be a revolution because they need it bad enough to die for it. They follow us because we know that, and because we don't lie to them. This is only the first battle, but it's starting, and we're winning. That's what's important—not Herth."

I stared at her. At last I said, "How long did it take you to memorize that?"

Fires burned behind her eyes and I was struck by a wave of anger and I badly wished I'd kept my mouth shut.

I said, "Cawti—"

She stood up, put on her cloak and walked out.

If Loiosh had said anything I'd probably have killed him.

9 —

. . .& polish.

I stayed up all night, walking around the neighborhood.
I wasn't completely nuts, the way I'd been before, but I
suppose I wasn't quite rational, either. I did try to be
careful and I wasn't attacked. Morrolan reached me
psionically at some point in there, but claimed it wasn't
important when I asked why, so I didn't find out what
he wanted. After a few hours I had calmed down a bit. I
thought about going home, but realized that I didn't
want to go home to an empty house. Then I realized that
I didn't want to go home to find Cawti waiting up for
me, either.

I sat down in an all-night klava hole and drank klava
until my kidneys cried for mercy. When daylight began
to filter down through the orange-red haze that
Dragaerans think is a sky, I still wasn't feeling sleepy. I
ate a couple of hen's eggs at a place I didn't know, then
wandered over to the office. That earned me a raised
eyebrow from Melestav.

I sniffed around the place and made sure that everything was running smoothly. It was. Once, some time
ago, I'd left the office in Kragar's hands for a few days
and he'd made an organizational disaster of the place,
but he seemed to have learned since then. There were a

couple of notes indicating people wanted to see me about business-type things, but they weren't urgent so I decided to let them sit. Then I reconsidered and gave them to Melestav with instructions to have Kragar check into them a little more. When someone wants to see you—and someone is after your head—it might be a set up. Just to satisfy your curiosity, they were both legitimate.

I would have dozed then but I was still too worked up. I went down to the lab and took off my cloak and my jerkin and cleaned up the place, which had needed it for some time. I threw all the old coals away, swept and even polished a bit. Then I coughed for a while from the dust in the air.

I went back upstairs, cleaned myself up and left the building. Loiosh preceded me, and we were very careful. I slowly walked over toward South Adrilankha, staying as alert as I could. It was just before noon.

I stopped and had a leisurely meal at a place that didn't like Easterners or didn't like Jhereg or both. They overcooked the kethna, didn't chill the wine, and the service was slow and just on the edge of rude. There wasn't a lot I could do about it since I was out of my area, but I did get even with them; I overtipped the waiter and overpaid for the meal. Let them wonder.

As I approached South Adrilankha on Wheelwright, I began to notice a certain amount of tension and excitement on the faces I passed. Yeah. Whatever these Easterners were doing, they were certainly doing it. I saw a pair of Phoenix Guards walking briskly the same way I was, and I became unobtrusive until they passed.

I stopped a couple of blocks from Carpenter to study things. The street here was quite wide, as this was a main road for goods from South Adrilankha. There were crowds of Dragaerans—Teckla and an occasional Orca or Jhegaala—milling around and either looking west or heading that way. I thought about sending Loiosh to take a look, but I didn't want to be separated from him for that long; there was still my presumed assassin to worry about. I moved west another block, but the street curved and I couldn't see Carpenter.

Have you ever seen a fight break out in an inn? Sometimes you know what's going on before you actually see the fight, because the guy next to you snaps his head around, half stands up, and stares, and then you see two or three people backing away from something that's hidden by someone else standing right in front of you. So you're suddenly all nerve endings, and you stand up and move back a bit, and that's when you see the brawlers.

Well, this was kind of like that. At the far end of the block, where it curved a little to the north, everyone was staring off toward Carpenter and having the kind of conversation where you keep looking at the object of interest instead of the person to whom you're talking. I noticed about five Dragaerans in Phoenix livery looking officious but not doing anything. I decided they were waiting for orders.

I walked that last block very slowly. I began to hear occasional shouts. When I got around the corner, all I could see was a wall of Dragaerans, lined up along Carpenter between the Grain Exchange and Molly's general store. There were a few more uniforms present. I did another check for possible assassins and began to move into the crowd.

"Boss?"

"Yeah?"

"What if he's in the crowd waiting for you?"

"You'll spot him before he gets to me."

"Oh. Well, that's all right then."

He had a point, but there was nothing I could do about it. Getting through a tightly packed group of people without being noticed is not one of the easiest things to do unless you happen to be Kragar. It took all of my concentration, which means I didn't have any to spare for someone trying to kill me. It's hard to describe how you go about it, yet it is something that can be learned. It involves a lot of little things, like keeping your attention focused in the same direction as everyone around you; it's amazing how much this helps. Sometimes you dig an elbow into someone's ribs because he'd notice you if you didn't. You have to catch the rhythm of the crowd and be part of it. I know that sounds funny, but it's the best I can do. Kiera the Thief taught me, and even she can't really explain it. But explanations don't matter. I got up to the front of the crowd without calling attention to myself; leave it at that. And once I was there I saw what the commotion was about.

I guess when I'd first heard Cawti speaking of putting up barricades, I'd sort of pictured it as finding a bunch of logs and laying them across the street high enough to keep people out. But it wasn't like that at all. The barricade seemed to have been built from anything someone didn't want. Oh, sure, there was a bit of lumber here and there, but that was only the start of it. There were several broken chairs, part of a large table, damaged garden tools, mattresses, the remains of a sofa, even a large porcelain washbasin with its drainpipe sticking up into the air.

It completely filled the intersection, and I saw a bit of smoke drifting up from behind it as if someone had a small fire going. There were maybe fifty on the other side watching the Dragaerans and listening to insults without responding. The Easterners and Teckla who manned the barricade had sticks, knifes and a few more swords than I'd seen the day before. Those on my side were unarmed. The Phoenix Guard—I saw about twenty—had their weapons sheathed. Once or twice a Dragaeran would look like he was about to climb the barricade and ten or fifteen Easterners would just go over there, opposite him, and stand close together, and he'd climb down again. When that happened, the uniforms would kind of watch closely, as if they were ready to move, but they'd relax again when the Dragaeran climbed down.

A cart, drawn by an ox, came down the street from the other side. It got about halfway down the block and three Easterners went over and talked to the driver, who was Dragaeran. They talked for a while, and I could hear that the driver was cursing, but eventually she turned around in the street and went back the way she came.

It was exactly as Cawti said: They weren't letting anyone either in or out of South Adrilankha. They had built a makeshift wall and, if that wasn't enough, the Easterners behind it were ready to deal with anyone who climbed over. No one was getting past them.

When I'd seen all I wanted to, I got past them and headed down the street toward Kelly's flat on the assumption that things must be popping there. I took my time though, and made a couple of detours to other streets that intersected Carpenter to see if things were the same. They were. Carpenter and Wheelwright had the biggest crowd, because that was the biggest and busiest intersection, but the others I checked were also locked up tight. I watched a few repetitions of scenes I'd already witnessed. This became boring so I left.

I made my twisting, winding way to my spot across from Kelly's flat, checked my weapons and began waiting. I'd been coming here every day for quite a while now, and following no other pattern. Unless I was completely wrong about Herth wanting to kill me (which I couldn't believe), the assassin would have to realize that this was his best shot. Unless he suspected a trap. Would I have suspected a trap? I didn't know.

There wasn't much activity at Kelly's. Paresh was standing outside, and so were a couple of Easterners I didn't recognize. People would enter and leave every so often, but there was no sign of the frenzied activities of the last few days. An hour and a little more slipped by this way, while I struggled to stay alert and ready. I was starting to feel fatigued from lack of sleep, which worried me; fatigued is not the best way to feel when you are expecting an attempt on your life. I also felt grimy and generally unclean, but that didn't bother me as it fit my mood.

The first sign that something was going on occurred when Cawti and Gregory showed up, hurrying, and disappeared into the headquarters. A few minutes later Gregory went running out again. I checked my weapons because it felt like the thing to do. Ten minutes later a group of about forty, led by Gregory, showed up and began hanging around the place.

Within a minute after that, four Phoenix Guards arrived and stationed themselves directly in front of Kelly's door. My mouth was suddenly very dry. Four Phoenix Guards and forty Easterners and Teckla, yet I was scared for the Easterners and Teckla.

I wondered if their presence meant that the barricades were down, or whether they'd broken the barricades, but then I realized that there were bound to be a large number of Guards stationed in South Adrilankha all the time. I guessed we'd be seeing more soon. Then I noticed something: of the four Guards, three of them wore clothing that was green, brown and yellow. I looked closer. Yes, these four Phoenix Guards consisted of three Teckla and a Dragon. This meant that the Empress was worried enough about this situation to use conscripted Teckla. I licked my lips.

Cawti appeared from within and began speaking to the Dragonlord. She still wore Jhereg colors and Rocza was riding on her left shoulder. I couldn't tell what effect she was having on him, but I assumed he wasn't going to be overflowing with good will.

They spoke for a while and his hand strayed to his sword hilt. I caught my breath. Another unbreakable Jhereg rule is, you *don't* kill Imperial Guards. On the other hand, it wasn't at all clear to me that I was going to have a choice. I am not so completely in control of myself as I would sometimes like to believe. Perhaps that is what I've learned from all of this.

The Guard didn't draw, however, he merely gripped his weapon. And Cawti could take care of herself, and the Guards were outnumbered ten to one. I reminded myself to stay alert for the presumed assassin.

Eight more Phoenix Guards showed up. Then another four. The ratio continued to be three Teckla for each Dragon. One from this last group had a brief conference with the fellow who'd been speaking to Cawti, then she—the new Guard—resumed negotiations. I guess she out-ranked the other one or something. About thirty more of Kelly's people appeared then, and you could almost feel the temperature in the area rise. I saw Cawti shake her head. They talked some more and Cawti shook her head again. I wanted to make contact with her—to say, hey, I'm here; is there something I can do? But I knew the answer already, and asking would only distract her.

Stay alert, Vlad, I told myself.

The Guard abruptly turned away from Cawti and I heard her issue her orders in a clear, crisp voice: "Back off thirty feet. Weapons sheathed, stay alert." The Guards followed her orders at once, the Dragons looking efficient and smart in their black uniforms, trimmed with silver, with the Phoenix breast insignia and gold half-cloak of the Phoenix. The Teckla who were Guards looked just a bit silly in their peasant outfits with Phoenix insignia and gold half-cloaks. They seemed to be trying to look calm. Cawti went back inside. Natalia and Paresh emerged and circulated among the Easterners, speaking to small groups of them. Pep talks, probably.

Twenty minutes later about forty or fifty more citizens arrived. All of these had knives that were long enough to be almost swords. They were well-muscled men and carried their knives like they knew how to use them. It occurred to me that they probably came from one of the slaughterhouses. Ten minutes after that, about twenty more Phoenix Guards showed up. This continued for most of another hour, with the street gradually filling up until I could no longer see the door to Kelly's flat. I could, however, see the Captain (or whatever; I didn't know what rank she was) of the Phoenix Guards. I had her face in half profile, about thirty feet away to my right. She reminded me just a bit of Morrolan—Dragon features—but she wasn't nearly as tall. I got the impression that she wasn't at all happy about this situation—there were only Teckla and Easterners to be fought, but there were a lot of them, on their home territory, and three-fourths of her forces were Teckla. I wondered what Kelly was up to. My guess (I was right, too) was that the Empress had learned who was behind all of this trouble and had sent her Guards to arrest him, and he had no intention of going.

Okay, but was he going to let a couple of hundred of his "people" die to prevent it? Sure, that made sense. He was following a principle; what did he care if people were killed? What puzzled me was that this wouldn't save him unless he won. Teckla or not, there were also Dragons among those Guards (and one Dzur, I noticed). Some of them were probably sorcerers. This could be a real bloodbath. Of course, Paresh was a sorcerer, and so was Cawti, but I didn't like the odds.

I was trying to puzzle this out when another group arrived. There were six of them surrounding a seventh and they were Dragaerans. They did not, however, represent the Empire. The six were obviously Jhereg bodyguard or muscle types. The seventh was Herth.

My palms became simultaneously itchy and sweaty. I knew I couldn't make a move right then and hope to live through it, but Verra! how I wanted to! I hadn't known that I had that much capacity for hate left in me until I saw this man who had had me tortured to the point where I had broken, and given them information to destroy a group my wife was willing to give her life for. It was as if he epitomized all of the bile I'd swallowed in my lifetime, and I stood there shaking and staring and hating.

Loiosh squeezed my shoulder. I tried to relax and stay alert for the assassin.

Herth spotted the captain and walked right up to her. A couple of Guards got in between them and Herth's bodyguards stepped in to face them and I wondered if I was going to see a different fight than the one I'd expected. But the captain pushed the other Guards aside and faced Herth. Herth stopped about twenty feet away from her and his bodyguards moved back. I had a perfect view of them both. I had a perfect shot at Herth.

I could have dropped two of those bodyguards with a pair of throwing knives, scattered the others with a handful of shuriken, and shined Herth before the Dragons could stop me. I couldn't have made it out alive, but I could have had him. Instead I squeezed into the corner of the building and watched and listened and cursed under my breath.

"Good afternoon, Lieutenant," said Herth. So I was wrong about her rank. So big deal.

"What do you want, Jhereg?" The Dragonlord's voice was clipped and harsh. I would almost guess she didn't like Jhereg.

"You seem to have a problem."

She spat. "In five minutes I won't anymore. Now clear out of here."

"I think I can arrange to have this problem solved peaceably, Lieutenant."

"I can arrange for you to be—"

"Unless you enjoy killing civilians. Maybe you do. I wouldn't know."

She stared at him for a while. Then she walked up and stood nose to nose with him. One of his bodyguards started forward. Herth gestured to him and he stopped. The lieutenant slowly and carefully drew a long fighting knife from a hip sheath next to her sword. Without removing her eyes from Herth's she tested it with her thumb. Then she showed it to him. Then she drew it along his cheek. First across one side, then the other. I could see lines of red where she'd cut him. He didn't flinch. When she was done, she wiped the blade on his cloak, put it away, and walked slowly away from him.

He said, "Lieutenant."

She turned. "Yes?"

"My offer still stands."

She considered him for a moment. "What's the offer?"

"Let me speak to this person, the one inside, and allow me to convince him to end this silly inland blockade."

She nodded slowly. "Very well, Ihereg. Their time is about up. I'll give you an additional ten minutes. Starting now."

Herth turned toward the door to Kelly's flat, but even as he did so I heard it swing open. (It was only then that I realized how quiet the street had become.) At first I couldn't see the door, but then the Easterners in front of it moved aside and I saw fat, little Kelly, with Paresh on one side of him and Cawti on the other. Paresh's attention was fixed on Herth, and his eyes were like daggers. Cawti was looking over the situation like a pro, and her black headband suddenly seemed incongruous. What really caught my attention, though, was that Herth's back was to me and there was only one bodyguard between us. It hurt to do nothing.

Kelly spoke first. "So," he said, "You are Herth." He was squinting so hard I couldn't see his eyes. His voice was clear and strong.

Herth nodded. "You must be Kelly. Shall we go inside and talk?"

"No," said Kelly flatly. "Anything you have to say to me, the whole world can hear, and the whole world can hear my answer, as well."

Herth shrugged. "All right. You can see the kind of situation you're in, I think."

"I can see it more clearly than either you or that friend of yours who cuts your face before granting your wishes."

That stopped him for a moment, then he said, "Well, I'm giving you a chance to live. If you remove—"

"The Phoenix Guard will not attack us."

Herth paused, then chuckled. The lieutenant, hearing this, looked amused.

Then I noticed Natalia, Paresh and two Easterners I didn't know. They were walking along the line of Phoenix Guards, handing each of them, even the Dragons, a piece of paper. The Dragons glanced at it and threw it away, the Teckla started talking to each other, and reading it aloud for those who couldn't read.

Herth paused to watch this drama, looking vaguely

troubled. The lieutenant matched his expression, except she seemed a bit angry. Then she said, "All right, that will be enough—"

"What's the problem, then?" asked Kelly in a loud voice. "What are you afraid they'll do if they read that?"

The lieutenant swung and stared at him, and they held that way for a moment. I caught a glimpse of the paper that someone had dropped and the breeze brought near me. It began, "BROTHERS—CONSCRIPTS" in large print. Underneath, before the breeze carried it away again, I read, "You, conscripted Teckla, are being incited against us, Easterners and Teckla. This plan is being put into operation by our common enemies, the oppressors, the privileged few—generals, bankers, landlords—"

The lieutenant turned away from Herth and grabbed one of the leaflets and read it. It was fairly long, so it took her awhile. As she read, she turned pale and I saw her jaw clench. She glanced over at her command, many of whom had broken formation and were clearly discussing the leaflet, some waving it about as if agitated.

At this moment Kelly began speaking, over Herth's head, as it were. He said, "Brothers! Conscripted Teckla! Your masters—the generals, the captains, the aristocrats—are preparing to throw you against us, who are organizing to fight them, to defend our right to a decent life—to walk the streets without fear. We say join us, for our cause is just. But if you don't, we warn you, don't let them send you against us, for the steel of our weapons is as cold as the steel of yours."

As he began to speak, Herth frowned and backed away. The whole time he was speaking, the lieutenant kept making motions toward him, as if she'd shut up him, then back toward her troops, as if to order them forward. When he stopped speaking at last, there was silence in the street.

I nodded. Whatever else I thought about Kelly, he'd handled this situation in a way I hadn't expected him to, and it seemed to be working. At least, the lieutenant didn't seem to quite know what to do.

Herth finally spoke. "Do you expect that to accomplish anything?" he asked. It seemed rather weak to me. To Kelly too, I guess, because he didn't answer. Herth said, "If you're done with your public speaking, and hope to avoid arrest or slaughter, I suggest that you and I try to make arrangements for—"

"You and I have nothing whatever to arrange. We want you and yours out of our neighborhoods entirely, and we won't rest until that is done. There is no basis for discussion between us."

Herth looked down at Kelly and I could imagine, although I couldn't see it, the cold smile on Herth's face. "Have it as you will then, Whiskers," he said. "No one can say I didn't try."

He turned and walked back toward the lieutenant.

Then I was distracted because someone else showed up. I didn't notice him at first because I was watching Kelly and Herth, but he must have been making his way along the street the entire time, past the Phoenix Guards and the Easterners, and right up to the door to Kelly's flat.

"Cawti!" came the voice as from nowhere. It was a voice I knew, though I can hardly think of one I less expected to hear at that moment.

I looked at Cawti. She, as amazed as I, was staring at the old, bald, frail Easterner who stood next to her. "We must speak," said my grandfather. I couldn't believe it. His voice, in the continuing silence that followed the confrontation between Herth and Kelly, carried all the way over to my side of the street. But was he going to start throwing our family business around? Now? In public? What was he up to?

"Noish-pa," she said. "Not now. Can't you see—?"

"I see much," he said. "Yes, now." He was leaning on a cane. I knew that cane. The top could be unscrewed to reveal—a sword? Heavens, no. He carried a rapier at his hip. The cane held four vials of Fenarian peach brandy. Ambrus was curled up on his shoulder and seemed no more upset by any of this than he was. Herth didn't know what to make of him, and a quick glance told me that the lieutenant was as puzzled as I was. She was biting her lip.

"We must go off the street so we can talk," said my grandfather.

Cawti didn't know what to say.

I began cursing anew under my breath. Now there was no question: I was going to have to do something. I couldn't let my grandfather be caught in the middle of this.

Then my attention was drawn back to the lieutenant, who shook herself and stood up straighter. Her troops seemed to still be in a state of some confusion, talking in animated tones about the flyer and Kelly's speech. The lieutenant turned toward the mob of Easterners and said in a loud voice, "Clear away, all of you." No one moved. She drew her blade, a strange one that curved the wrong way, like a scythe. Kelly locked eyes with Herth. Cawti's gaze shifted among the lieutenant, my grandfather, Kelly and Herth. I let a dagger fall into my hand, wondering what I could do with it.

The lieutenant hesitated, studied her troops, then called out, "Weapons at ready." There was some sound of steel being drawn as the Dragons did so, and a few of the Teckla. The Easterners gripped their weapons and moved forward, forming a solid wall. A few more of the Guard drew weapons. I spared Kelly a glance and he was looking at my grandfather, who was looking at him. They exchanged nods, as of old acquaintances. Interesting.

My grandfather drew his rapier. He said to Cawti, "This is no place for you."

"Padraic Kelly," called the lieutenant in a piercing voice, "I arrest you in the name of the Empress. Come with me at once."

"No," said Kelly. "Tell the Empress that unless she agrees to a full investigation into the murders of our comrades, by tomorrow there will be no clear road into or out of the city, and by the following day the docks will be closed. And if she attacks us now, the Empire will fall by morning.''

The lieutenant called, ''Forward!'' and the Phoenix Guard took a step toward the Easterners and I knew what I could use the dagger for. This was because in a single instant Kelly, my grandfather, and even Cawti were swept out of my mind. Everyone's attention was focused on the advancing Guards and the Easterners. Everyone's, that is, except mine. My attention was focused on Herth's back, about forty feet away from me.

Now he was mine. Even his bodyguards were all but ignoring him. Now I could take him and be away, cleanly. It was as if my entire life were about to be fulfilled in one thrust of an eight-inch stiletto.

Out of habit from the last four days, I gave myself a last caution before I moved away from the wall. Then I took a step toward Herth, holding the knife low against my body.

Then Loiosh screamed in my mind and there was suddenly a knife coming at my throat. It was attached to a Dragaeran who wore the colors of House Jhereg.

The assassin had finally made his move.

10-

1 grey silk cravat: repair cut. . .

The fact that I was ready for him did nothing to prevent the cold sweat that broke out all over me when I saw him. For one thing, he was ready for me, too, and he had the jump. All thought of Herth was instantly gone, replaced by thoughts of survival.

Sometimes, in this kind of situation, time slows down. Other times it speeds up, and I'm only aware of what I'm doing after I've done it. This was one of the former. I had time to see the knife come toward my throat, and to decide on a countering move, make it, and sit back wondering if it would work. While disarming myself is never my favorite thing to do in a fight, it was my only option. I flipped my knife at him, jumped the other way, and hit the ground rolling. I kept moving as I came up in case he decided to throw some pointy things at me, too. As it happened, he did, and one of them—a knife, I think—came close enough to make the hair on my neck stand up. But I avoided everything else long enough to draw my rapier. As I did so, I told Loiosh, *"I can handle this; take care of Cawti."*

"Right, boss." And I heard him flap-flap away.

That was actually one of the biggest lies I've ever told, but I was very much aware that mayhem was going to be breaking out around me when the Easterners clashed with the Phoenix Guards, and I didn't want to be distracted by worrying about Cawti.

Around then, as I came to a guard position, I realized that Herth's bodyguards had shots at my back, and that there were more than seventy Phoenix Guards there, any of whom might look over this way in between cutting down Easterners. I licked my lips, felt scared, and concentrated on the man before me—a professional killer who had accepted money to kill me.

I took my first good look at the assassin. A nondescript sort of guy with maybe a trace of the Dzur in the slant of his eyes and the point of chin. He had long straight hair with a neat widow's peak. *Points all over the bastard*, I thought. His eyes were clear and light brown and his glance strayed over me, studying. If things weren't going as he planned (which, I guarantee, they weren't) it didn't show in his expression.

He'd drawn a sword by this time. He was standing full forward with a heavy rapier in his right hand and a long fighting knife in his left. I presented only my side, as my grandfather had taught me. I closed with him before he could throw anything else at me, stopping when we were point-to-point—that is, just at the distance from each other where the points of our blades could barely touch. From here, the concentration he'd need for a good windup with that knife would give me time to get in at least one good cut or thrust, which would settle the issue if I was lucky.

I wondered if he were a sorcerer. I glanced at his knife but didn't see anything to indicate that it was a magical weapon. Not that there had to be anything to see. My hands were sweaty. I remembered that my grandfather had recommended light gloves for fencing, for just that reason. I resolved to get some if I lived through this.

He made a tentative pass, either recognizing or knowing that I fought strangely and trying to get a feel for my style. He wasn't as fast as I'd feared, so I placed a light cut on his right hand to teach him to keep his distance.

It was frightening to be having this kind of fight with

Phoenix Guards in the area, but they were all involved in the slaughter of Easterners and were thus too busy to notice us—

No, they weren't.

I realized quite suddenly that five or six seconds had passed and there were no sounds of battle.

He didn't realize it yet and tried rushing me then. He did a fine job of it, too. There was no warning that he was about to go, and the timing of his slash, at an angle from my right to left, was very good. I avoided the attack, letting his blade slide up mine, screeching, until I could deflect it. I noted his speed. He had a certain grace, too; the kind that came with long training. And he was utterly passionless. From looking at his face, I couldn't tell if he was confident, worried, gleeful, or what.

I made a halfhearted riposte, trying to figure out how to get out of this situation. I mean, I would have loved to finalize him, but not with the Phoenix Guard looking on, and it wasn't at all clear that I could manage to in any case. He blocked my riposte with his dagger. I decided that he probably wasn't a sorcerer, since sorcerers like to use enchanted daggers for spell-casting, and no one likes to parry with enchanted cutlery.

He kept coming up on the ball of his right foot and tensing his left leg. I resolved not to let it distract me. I kept my attention on his eyes. No matter how you're fighting, sword, spell, or empty-handed, your opponent's eyes are your first indication of when he'll move.

There was a second or two of inaction, during which I would have loved to have launched an attack but didn't dare. Then, I guess, he realized that there were no sounds of battle from around us. Without warning he bounded back a couple of steps, a couple more, then turned and walked briskly away, disappearing around the corner of a building.

I stood there breathing heavily for just a moment, then I suddenly thought of Herth again. If he'd been in sight I probably would have shined him, Phoenix Guard or no. But when I turned around I didn't see him.

Loiosh landed on my shoulder.

The two lines, Kelly's group and the Phoenix Guards, faced each other about ten feet apart. Most of the Guards seemed very unhappy about the situation. Kelly's people seemed solid and determined; a human wall with knives and sticks bristling from it like thorns from a vine.

I was alone in the middle of the street, about sixty feet to the side of the Phoenix Guards, some of whom were looking at me. Most of them, however, watched their lieutenant. She was holding her peculiar blade over her head, parallel to the ground in a gesture that suggested "hold," or perhaps, "sit," "stay," or "heel."

Cawti stood next to my grandfather and they were staring at me. I sheathed my sword so I wouldn't be as interesting. The Easterners were still watching the Guards, most of whom were watching their lieutenant. She, at least, hadn't seen me. I moved to a slightly more open part of the street so the assassin couldn't come back at me without giving me time to react. Then the lieutenant spoke in a voice that carried quite well, although it seemed that she wasn't shouting. She said, "I have received communication from the Empress. All troops back off to the other side of the street and stand ready."

The Phoenix Guard did so, the Teckla happily, the Dragons less so. I'll say this for Kelly: He didn't gloat. He just stood watching everything with his jowl set. I mean, it didn't surprise me that much that he didn't look relieved; I might have been able to manage that. But keeping the gloat off my face when the troops pulled back would have been beyond me.

I made my way over to where my family stood. I couldn't read Cawti's expression. My grandfather said, "He was pressing you, Vladimir. If he had continued, he would have had the initiative and your balance would have been not right."

"Pressing me?"

"Each time he shifted his feet, he would end with his weight more forward. It is a trick some of these elfs use.

I think they don't know they are doing it."

I said, "I'll remember, Noish-pa."

"But you were careful, which is good, and your wrist was supple but firm, as it should be, and you didn't linger after the stop-cut, as you used once to do."

"Noish-pa—," said Cawti.

"Thank you," I said.

"You shouldn't be here," said Cawti.

"And why should I not?" he said. "What is there to this life that is so worth saving?"

Cawti glanced around as if to see who was listening to us. I did, too. No one seemed to be.

"But why?"

"Why am I here? Cawti, I don't know. I know that I cannot change how you are, or what you will do. I know that girls aren't the same in Faerie as back home, and do what they want to, and that is not always a bad thing. But I came to tell you that you can come to see me if you want, and if you want to talk about things, yes? Vladimir, he comes now and then when he is troubled, but you don't. That is all I have to say. Yes?"

She looked at him for a moment, and I saw there were tears in her eyes. She leaned forward and kissed him. "Yes, Noish-pa," she said. Ambrus meowed. My grandfather smiled with what was left of his teeth, turned, walked away, leaning on his cane. I stood next to Cawti watching him. I tried to think of something to say but couldn't.

Cawti said, "Now we know why he was here; why were you here?"

"I was trying to convince that assassin to do just what he did. The idea was for me to shine him."

She nodded. "You've marked him?"

"Yeah. I'll set Kragar to work on it."

"So you know he has your name, and you'll have his, and you'll be trying to kill each other. What do you think he'll do now?"

I shrugged.

Cawti said, "What would you do?"

I shrugged again. "Dunno. Either return the money

and run as far and as fast as I can, or move right away. Within the day, maybe within the hour. Try to catch the guy before he could set things up."

She nodded. "Me, too. Do you want to drop out of sight?"

"Not especially. There are—"

The lieutenant began speaking again. "All citizens harken. The following words are from the Empress: You are hereby informed that a full investigation, as you . . . requested, is and has been taking place in accordance with Imperial procedure. You are ordered to disband at once and remove all obstructions from the street. No arrests will take place if these things are done."

Then she turned and faced her troops. "Return to duty. That is all." The Guards resheathed their weapons. The reactions from the Guards were interestingly diverse. Some of the Dragons gave us looks that read, "You're lucky this time, scum," and others were mildly regretful, as if they had been looking forward to the exercise. The Teckla seemed relieved. The lieutenant didn't spare us another look or gesture, she simply rejoined her unit and walked away.

I turned back to Cawti, but as I did Paresh touched her on the shoulder and gestured to the headquarters. Cawti reached out and squeezed my arm once before following him. As she was disappearing, Rocza left her shoulder and landed on mine.

"Someone thinks I need help, boss."

"Yeah. Or I do. Do you mind?"

"Naw. I can use the company. You've been too quiet lately. I've been getting lonely."

I didn't have an answer for that.

I didn't take any chances going back to the office; I teleported, then went inside to be sick rather than waiting in the street.

"Any luck with Herth, Kragar?"

"I'm working on it, boss."

"Okay. I've got another face. Ready?"

"What do you mean—Oh. Okay. Go ahead."

I gave him the image of the assassin. I said, "Know him?"

"No. Do you have a name?"

"No. I want one."

"Okay. I'll have a picture made and see what I can find."

"And when you find him, don't waste time asking me. Have him sent for a walk." Kragar raised an eyebrow at me. I said, "He's the one who's got my name. He almost had my head today, too."

Kragar whistled. "How'd you get out of it?"

"I was ready for it. I guessed someone was after me, so I gave him a pattern to my movements to sucker him out."

"And then you didn't manage to shine him?"

"A little matter of seventy or eighty Phoenix Guards in the area. Also, he wasn't as surprised as I'd hoped, and he was pretty good with a blade."

Kragar said, "Oh."

"So now I know what he looks like, but not his name."

"And so you give me the fun part, huh? All right. Do you have anyone in mind?"

"Yeah. Mario. If you can't find him, use someone else."

Kragar rolled his eyes. "Nothing like specific instructions. All right."

"And bring me a new set of weapons. Might as well do something with my hands while I wait for you to solve all my problems for me."

"Not all of them, Vlad. I can't do anything about your height."

"Go."

He went out and left me with Loiosh, Rocza, and my thoughts. I realized I was hungry and thought about having someone bring me some food. Then it occurred to me that I was going to be teleporting everywhere for a while now, so maybe that wasn't a good idea. Loiosh and Rocza hissed back and forth, then started chasing each other around the room until I opened the window and told them to do it outside. I was very careful to stand to the side when I opened it. I don't know of an assassin who would choose to try to get someone from across a street, but the guy was probably pretty desperate by now. At least, I would have been. I shut the window and drew the drapes.

I could at least accomplish a few things that I'd been too busy for.

"Melestav!"

"Yeah?"

"Is Sticks in the office today?"

"Yes."

"Send him up here."

"Right."

A few minutes later Sticks sauntered in and I handed him a purse with fifty Imperials in it. He weighed it without counting it and looked at me. "What's this for?"

I said, "Shut up."

He said, "Oh. That. Well, thanks." He sauntered out again.

Kragar came back in with a new set of toys for me. I shut the door after him and set up about changing weapons. I took off my cloak and began removing things from it and replacing them as I went. When the cloak was done I starting digging things out of the ribbing of my jerkin and other places. While I was removing the dagger from my left sleeve, I noticed Spellbreaker. I guess I'd been avoiding thinking about it since that night, but now I let it fall into my hand.

It hung there, just like an ordinary chain. I studied it. It was about eighteen inches long, golden, made of thin links. The gold didn't seem to be plating; it had never scratched or anything. But the chain didn't seem heavy enough for solid gold, and it certainly wasn't soft. I tried digging a fingernail into one of the links and it felt like a fine steel.

I decided that I really ought to try to find out what I could about the thing, if I lived through this. I continued changing weapons while I thought about that. What would it take to live through this?

Well, I'd have to kill the assassin, that was certain. And Herth. No, correct that: I was going to have to kill Herth *before* I killed the assassin, or Herth would just hire another one. I thought about hiring someone to kill Herth. That would be the intelligent thing to do. For one thing, then I'd know that he'd go down even if I did. And I still had all of that cash lying around; more than I'd ever dreamed of having. If Mario decided to show up and walk into my office, I could even meet his figure.

The trouble was, not many assassins besides Mario would agree to take on the job. Herth was a boss—a much bigger one than I. He was the kind who doesn't take a pee without four or five bodyguards there in case his pecker decides to attack him. Shining someone like that requires getting to at least one or two of his body-guards, or Mario, or finding someone who doesn't mind dying, or a great deal of luck.

I could forget Mario; no one even knew where he was. Maybe Kelly knew someone who wanted to make a suicide attack on a Jhereg boss, but I don't hang around with that sort of individual. Getting to his bodyguards might be possible, but it takes time. You have to find the ones who will take, check them out afterwards to make sure they've taken, and set up a time when both you and they can do it with a minimum of risk. I didn't have that kind of time before the assassin made another attack.

That left luck. Did I feel lucky? No, I didn't.

So where did that leave me?

Dead.

I finished changing weapons while I thought about it. I looked at it from a few other angles. Could I somehow convince Herth to cease hostilities? Laughable. Especially since I *still* had to make sure he wouldn't kill Cawti. I mean, that's what had gotten me into this mess, I might as well—

Was it? Is that why I'd gotten involved in all of this

nonsense? Well, no, not at first; at first I had wanted to
find the murderer of this Franz fellow whom I'd never
met. I'd wanted to do that to help patch things up with
Cawti. Shit. Why was *I* trying to patch things up with
her? She was the one who'd gotten involved in all this
without mentioning it to me. Why did I have to go sticking my nose into a place where I wasn't wanted and I
didn't want to be? Duty? A pretty word, that. Duty.
Doo-tee. Easterners—some of them—made it sound
like doo-dee; the kind of thing you hum to yourself
while changing weapons. Doo-dee-da-dee-dee-do. What
did it mean?

Maybe "duty" can't just hang there in a void; maybe
it has to be attached to something. A lot of Easterners
attached it to Barlan, or Verra, or Crow, or one of the
other gods. I couldn't do that; I'd been around Dragaerans too long and I'd picked up their attitudes toward
gods. What else was there? The Jhereg? Don't make me
laugh. My duty toward the Jhereg is to follow its rules
so I don't get shined. The Empire? My duty toward the
Empire is to make sure it doesn't notice me.

That left it pretty small. Family, I guess. Cawti, my
grandfather, Loiosh, and Rocza. Sure. That was a duty,
and one I could be proud to do. I thought about how
empty I'd felt before Cawti came into my life, and even
the memory was painful. Why wasn't that enough?

I wondered if Cawti had felt this way. She didn't have
the organization; she just had me. She used to have a
partner and they'd needed each other, but her partner
had become a Dragonlord and heir to the Orb. Now
what did she have? Was that why she'd gotten involved
with Kelly's people? To give her something to do, so
she'd feel useful? Wasn't I enough?

No. Of course not. No one can live his life through
someone else, I knew that. So what did Cawti have to
live for? She had her "people." This group of Easterners and an occasional Teckla who got together to talk
about overthrowing the Empire. Cawti hung around
with them, helped build barricades in the streets, stood
up to Phoenix Guards, and came home convinced that

she'd done her "duty." Maybe that's what duty was—
something you do to make yourself feel useful.

Fine. That was Cawti. Where was *my* duty? Doo-
deedle-deedle-dee. My duty was to die, because I was
going to anyway, so I might as well call it a duty. You're
getting cynical, Vlad, stop it.

I had about finished changing my weapons so I just
sat there, holding a dagger that was destined for my
right boot. I leaned back and closed my eyes. All of this
was really beside the point if I was going to be killed
soon. Or was it? Was there something I ought to be
doing, even if I were dying? Now that would be a good
test of "duty," whatever I meant by it.

And I realized there was. I had gotten myself involved
in this thing up to my neck mostly with the idea of keeping Cawti alive. If it was really as clear as all that that I
was going to die, I'd have to make sure that Cawti was
safe before I let anyone kill me.

Now there was a pretty little problem.

Doo-dee-deedee-dee-dum. I started flipping the dagger.

11 =

. . .and remove sweat stains

A little later, with the seeds of an idea taking shape in my head, I called for Kragar, but Melestav said he was out. I gnashed mental teeth and kept thinking. What, I wondered, would happen if I was killed and Cawti wasn't? My cynical half said it wouldn't be my problem. But beyond that, I guessed that my grandfather and Cawti would be able to look out for each other. There had been some sort of communication going on between them on the street there, something that had left me out. Were they going to get together and talk about how terrible I was? Was I going to die of paranoia?

Ignoring all of that, however, Cawti would be faced with an interesting problem if Herth killed me: She'd want to kill Herth herself, but she didn't want to be an assassin any more. Or at least, after the way she'd spoken to me I assumed she didn't want to be an assassin any more. On the other hand, it couldn't hurt Kelly any to have his biggest enemy taken off the stage. Too bad I'd have to die to pull it off. Hmmm.

I idly wondered whether there would be a way to convince Cawti I was dead long enough for her to kill Herth. My reappearance afterward would certainly be fun. On the other hand, it could get very embarrassing if

134

she chose not to go after him, and even more embarrassing if Herth found out I was alive.

Still, no need to dismiss it out of hand. It was better—

"You're looking morbid again, Vlad."

I didn't jump. "How kind of you to say so, Kragar. Anything on Herth?" He shook his head. I continued, "All right, a couple of thoughts have been buzzing around my head. I want to let one of them keep buzzing. The other one is to set things up to do it the long way."

"Buy off his protection?"

I nodded.

"Okay," he said. "I'll get started on it."

"Good. What about the assassin?"

"The artist should be just about finished. He said I have a very good mind for detail. Since I got the image from you, I think you ought to be flattered."

"Okay, I'm flattered. You know what to do with the picture."

He nodded and left and I went back to planning my death—or at least thinking about it. It seemed completely impractical, but tempting anyway. The triumphant return was what sounded best, I suppose. Of course, that wouldn't work too well if by the time I returned Cawti was shacking up with Gregory or someone.

I held that thought, just to see how much it bothered me. It more or less didn't, which somehow bothered me.

Loiosh and Rocza scratched on the window. I put the dagger I'd been flipping in its sheath and let them in. I stayed to the side, just in case. They seemed a bit exhausted.

"Sightseeing?"

"Yeah."

"Who won the race?"

"What makes you think we were racing, boss?"

"I didn't say you were; I just asked who won."

"Oh. She did. Wingspan."

"Yeah, that'll do it. I don't suppose you went anywhere near South Adrilankha, did you?"

"As a matter of fact we did."

"Ah. And the barricades?"

"Gone."

Loiosh settled on my shoulder. I sat down and said, *"A while ago you asked me what I'd think of Kelly's group if Cawti weren't involved."*

"Yeah."

"I've been thinking about it. I decided it doesn't matter. She is involved, and I have to work with things on that basis."

"Okay."

"And I think I know what I have to do about it."

He didn't say anything. I could feel him picking moods and random thoughts out of my brain. After a moment he said, *"Do you really think you're going to die?"*

"Yes and no. I guess I don't really believe it. I mean, we've been in situations before that have seemed this bad or worse. Mellar was tougher and smarter than Herth and the situation was worse. But I don't see how to get out of this one. I haven't been operating very well lately; maybe that's part of it."

"I know. So, what is it you're going to do?"

"Save Cawti. I don't know about the rest, but I have to do that much."

"Okay. How?"

"I can only think of two ways: One is to wipe out Herth, and probably his whole organization, so no one else can pick up the pieces and carry on."

"That doesn't seem too likely."

"No. The other way is arrange things so that Herth has no reason to go after Cawti."

"That sounds better. How do you plan to do it?"

"By wiping out Kelly and his little band myself."

Loiosh didn't say anything. From what I could pick up of his thoughts, he was too amazed to speak. I thought it a rather clever idea myself. After a while Loiosh said, *"But Cawti—"*

"I know. If you can think of a way for me to con-

vince both Cawti and Herth that I've died, that might
work too."

"Nothing comes to mind, boss. But—"

"Then let's get to work."

"I don't like this."

"Protest noted. Let's get busy. I want to have it over
with tonight."

"Tonight."

"Yeah."

"Okay, boss. Whatever you say."

I took out a piece of paper and started making a
diagram of everything I remembered in Kelly's place,
making notes where I wasn't sure of something, and trying to make guesses about back windows and so on.
Then I stared at it and tried to decide how to handle
things.

This could not, by any stretch of the imagination, be
called an assassination. It would be more like a slaughter. I was going to have to kill Kelly for certain, because
if he survived I wouldn't have accomplished anything.
Then Paresh, because he was a sorcerer; then as many
of the others as possible. There was no point in even trying to plan this out in the kind of detail I usually use;
not when trying to shine five or more at once.

The thought of a fire or explosion crossed my mind,
but I rejected the idea; buildings were too closely packed
there. I didn't want to burn down all of South Adrilankha.

I picked up the diagram and studied it. There was certainly going to be a back entrance to the building, and
probably a back entrance to the flat. I'd been quite a
ways into it and hadn't seen a kitchen, and Kelly's
private office had two doorways, so I could probably
start in back and work my way forward, to make sure
no one was awake in that part of the house. Since
everyone seemed to sleep in that front area, I would end
there, cut Kelly's throat, then Paresh's. If everyone else
was still sleeping by then, I would take them one at a
time. I wouldn't have to worry about revivifications,

since these were Easterners with no money, but if I could I'd go back and make sure anyway. Then I'd leave.

South Adrilankha would wake up tomorrow and these people would be gone. Cawti would be very upset, but she couldn't put the organization back together just by herself. At least, I hoped she couldn't. There were several other Easterners and Teckla involved in this, but the core would be gone and I didn't think those who remained would be able to do anything that could threaten Herth.

I studied the diagram then destroyed it. I leaned back in my chair, closed my eyes, went over the details, making sure I hadn't left anything out.

I got to Kelly's building halfway between midnight and dawn. The front door was only a curtain. I went around to the back. There was something of a door there, but it had no lock. I carefully and thoroughly oiled the hinges, and entered. This put me at the back of the building in a narrow hallway outside of Kelly's flat. Rocza was nervous on my right shoulder. I asked Loiosh to keep her quiet and soon she settled down.

I looked down the hall but couldn't see the front door—or anything else, for that matter. I have pretty fair night vision, but there are those who see better than I do. *"Is there anyone in the hall, Loiosh?"*

"No one, boss."

"Okay. Where's the back entrance to the flat?"

"Right here. If you put your hand out to the right you'll touch it."

"Oh."

I slipped past the curtain and was inside. I smelled food, some of it probably edible. There was certainly the stink of rotting vegetables.

After waiting a moment to check for the sounds of breathing, I risked a small sorcerous light from the tip of my forefinger. Yes, I was in a kitchen, and a bigger one than I'd expected. There were a few cupboards, an ice-chest, a pump. I lowered the light just a bit, held my forefinger in front of me and headed toward the front room.

I passed through the room where I'd spoken with Kelly. It was pretty much as I remembered it, except for a few more boxes. On one of them I caught the glitter of steel. I looked closer and saw a long dagger, which I recognized as the murder weapon—or else one very much like it. I checked it closer. Yeah, that was it.

I was starting to go past it into the next room, the library, when I sensed someone behind me. Trying to remember this now, it seems to me that Rocza tightened her grip on my shoulder just at that moment, but Loiosh didn't notice anything. In any case, my reaction to such things is foreordained: I spun, twisting a bit to the side, and drew a dagger from inside my cloak.

At first I didn't see anything, yet I continued to feel that there was someone in the room with me. I let the light from my forefinger fail and moved to the side, thinking that if I couldn't see him, there was no reason to let him see me. Then I became aware of a faint outline, as if there were a transparent figure in front of me. I didn't know what this meant, but I knew it wasn't normal. I let Spellbreaker fall into my left hand.

The figure didn't move, but it gradually grew more substantial, and it occurred to me that the room was dark as Verra's hair and I shouldn't be able to see anything.

"Loiosh, what do you see?"

"I'm not sure, boss."

"But you do see something."

"I think so."

"Yeah. Me, too." Rocza stirred uneasily. Well, I didn't blame her. Then I realized what I must be seeing and I blamed her even less.

It had been made pretty clear to me that I wasn't welcome, the time I walked the Paths of the Dead with Aliera and visited the Halls of Judgment. It was a place for the souls of Dragaerans, not the living bodies of Easterners. In order to arrive there, a body had to be

sent over Deathgate Falls (which would certainly insure
it was a corpse even it hadn't been before). Then it
floated down the river, fetching up somewhere along a
stretch of bank, from which the soul could travel—but
never mind that now. If the soul handled things right, it
would reach the Halls of Judgment, and unless some
god especially liked or disliked the guy, he'd take his
place as part of a thriving community of dead persons.

All right, fine.

What might happen to him if he isn't brought to
Deathgate Falls? Well, if he was killed with a Morganti
dagger, the issue was settled. Or, if he'd worked out
some arrangement with his favorite god, then the god
had the pleasure of doing anything he wanted with the
soul. Other than that, he'd be reincarnated. You don't
have to believe me, of course, but some recent expe-
riences have convinced me that this is fact.

Now, most of what I know about reincarnation I
learned from Aliera before I believed in it, so I've
forgotten a great deal of what she said. But I remember
that an unborn child exerts a kind of mystical pull and
will draw in the soul most suited to it. If no soul is ap-
propriate, there will be no birth. If there is no child ap-
propriate to a soul, the soul waits in a place that the
necromancers call "The Plane of Waiting Souls" because they aren't very imaginative. Why does it wait
there? Because it can't help it. There is something about
the place that pulls at the Dragaeran soul.

But what about Easterners? Well, it's pretty much the
same, as far as I can tell. When it comes down to a soul,
there just isn't that much difference between a Dragaeran and an Easterner. We aren't allowed into the
Paths of the Dead, but Morganti weapons have the
same effect on us, and we can make deals with any god
who feels like it, and we're probably reincarnated if
there's nothing else going on, or at least that's what the
Eastern poet-seer, Yain Cho Lin, is reported to have
said. In fact, according to the *Book of the Seven
Wizards,* the Plane of Waiting Souls pulls at us while
we're waiting, just like it does Dragaerans.

The book says, however, that it doesn't pull quite as hard. Why? Population. There are more Easterners in the world, so there are fewer souls waiting for places to go, so there are fewer souls to help call the others. Does this make sense? Not to me, either, but there it is.

One result of this weaker pull is that, sometimes, the soul of an Easterner will be neither reincarnated nor will it go to the Plane of Waiting Souls. Instead it will, well, just sort of hang around.

At least, that's the story. Believe it or not, as you choose.

I believe it, myself.

I was seeing a ghost.

I stared at it. Staring seems to be the first thing one does when seeing a ghost. I wasn't quite sure what the second thing ought to be. According to the stories my grandfather had told me when I was young, screaming was highly thought of. But if I screamed I'd wake up everyone in the place, and I needed them to be sleeping if I was going to kill them. Also, I didn't feel the urge. I knew I was supposed to be frightened, but when it came down to it, I was much more fascinated than scared.

The ghost continued to solidify. It was a bit luminescent, which was how I could see it. It was emitting a very faint blue glow. As I watched, I began to see the lines of its face. Soon I could tell that it was an Easterner, then that it was male. It seemed to be looking at me—that is, actually seeing me. Since I didn't want to wake everyone up, I moved out of the room, back into Kelly's study. I made a light again and navigated the floor to his desk and sat down. I don't know how I knew the ghost would follow me, but I did and he did.

I cleared my throat. "Well," I said. "You must be Franz."

"Yes," said the ghost. Can I say his voice was sepulchral? I don't care. It was.

"I'm Vladimir Taltos—Cawti's husband."

The ghost—no, let me just call him Franz. Franz nodded. "What are you doing here?" As he spoke he continued to solidify, and his voice became more normal.

"Well," I said. "That's a bit hard to explain. What are *you* doing here?"

His brow (which I could now see) came together. "I'm not sure," he said. I studied him. His hair was light, straight, and neatly combed. How does a ghost comb his hair? His face was pleasant but undistinctive, his demeanor had that honest and sincere look that I associate with spice salesmen and dead lyorn. He had a peculiar way of standing, as if he were leaning ever so slightly forward, and when I spoke he turned his head just a bit to the side. I wondered if he was hard of hearing, or just very intent on catching everything that was said. He seemed to be a very intense listener. In fact, he seemed intense just in general. He said, "I was standing outside the meeting hall—"

"Yes. You were assassinated."

"Assassinated!"

I nodded.

He stared at me, then looked at himself, then closed his eyes for a moment. Finally he said, "I'm dead now? A ghost?"

"Something like that. You should be waiting for reincarnation, if I understand how these things work. I guess there aren't any pregnant Easterners around here who quite fit the bill. Be patient."

He studied me, sizing me up.

"You're Cawti's husband."

"Yes."

"You say I was assassinated. We know what you do. Could it have been—"

"No. Or rather, it could have but it wasn't. A fellow named Yerekim did it. You people were getting in the way of a guy named Herth."

"And he had me killed?" Franz suddenly smiled. "To try to scare us off?"

"Yeah."

He laughed. "I can guess how well it worked for him. We organized the whole district, didn't we? Using my murder as a rallying point?"

I stared. "Good guess. It doesn't bother you?"

"Bother me? We've been trying to unite Easterners and Teckla against the Empire all along. Why would it bother me?"

I said, "Oh. Well, it seems to be working."

"Good." His expression changed. "I wonder why I'm back."

I said, "What do you remember?"

"Not much. I was just standing there and my throat started itching. Then I felt someone touch my shoulder from behind. I turned around and my knees felt weak and then . . . I don't know. I remember waking up, sort of, and feeling . . . worried, I guess. How long ago did it happen?"

I told him. His eyes widened. "I wonder what brought me back?"

"You say you felt worried?"

I nodded.

I sighed inaudibly. I had a good guess what had brought him back, but I chose not to share it with him.

"Hey, boss."

"Yeah."

"This is really weird."

"No it isn't. It's normal. Everything is normal. It's just that some normal things are weirder than other normal things."

"Oh. That explains it then."

Franz said, "Tell me what's happened since I died."

I complied, being as honest as I could. When I told him about Sheryl his face grew hard and cold and I remembered that I was dealing with a fanatic. I tightened my grip on Spellbreaker but continued the recitation. When I told him about the barricades a gleam came into his eye, and I wondered just how effective Spellbreaker would be.

"Good," he said when I'd finished. "We have them running now."

"Um, yeah," I said.

"Then it was worth it."

"Dying?"

"Yes."

"Oh."

"I should talk to Pat if I can. Where is everyone else?"

I almost told him they were asleep, but I caught myself. "I'm not sure," I said.

His eyes narrowed. "You're here alone?"

"Not at all," I said. Loiosh hissed to emphasize the point. He glanced at the two jhereg, but didn't smile. He seemed to have as big a sense of humor as the others. I added, "I'm sort of watching the place."

His eyes widened. "You've joined us?"

"Yes."

He smiled at me, and there was so much warmth in his expression that I would have kicked him, only he was incorporeal. "Cawti didn't think you would."

"Yeah, well."

"Exciting, isn't it?"

"Exciting. Yes, it certainly is that."

"Where's the latest issue?"

"Issue?"

"Of the paper."

"Oh. Um . . . it's around here somewhere."

He looked around the office, which I was still lighting up with my finger, and finally found one. He tried to pick it up, couldn't, kept trying, and finally managed. Then he set it down. "It's hard to hold things," he said. "Do you suppose you could turn the pages for me?"

"Uh, sure."

So I turned pages for him, and grunted agreement when he said things like, "No, he's missing the point," and, "Those bastards! How can they do that?" After a while he stopped and looked at me. "It was worth dying, but I wish I could be back in it again. There's so much to be done."

He went back to reading. I noticed that he seemed to be fading. I watched for a while, and the effect continued slowly but detectably. I said, "Look, I want to find people and let them know you're around, all right?

Can you sort of keep an eye on things? I'm sure if anyone comes in you can scare him to death."

He smiled. "All right. Go ahead."

I nodded and went back out the way I'd come,
through the kitchen and out the door.

"I thought we were going to kill them all, boss."

"So did I."

*"Couldn't you have gotten rid of the ghost with
Spellbreaker?"*

"Probably."

"Well then, why—"

"He's already been killed once too often."

"But what about the rest of them?"

"I changed my mind."

"Oh. Well, I didn't like the idea anyway."

"Good."

I teleported to a point a block from my house. There
were lamps in the street that provided enough light to
tell me I was alone. I made my way home very carefully,
checking for the assassin.

"Why did you change your mind, boss?"

*"I don't know. I have to think about it some more.
Something about Franz, I guess."*

I made my way up the stairs and into the house. The
sounds of Cawti's gentle breathing came from the bedroom. I removed my boots and cloak, then went in,
undressed, and climbed into bed carefully so I wouldn't
wake her.

As I closed my eyes I saw Franz's face before me. It
took longer than it should have to fall asleep.

12-

1 plain grey cloak: clean & press

I slept late and woke up slowly. I sat up in bed and tried to organize my thoughts and decide how to spend the day. My latest great scheme hadn't worked at all, so I went back to an earlier one. Was there any way, really, to convince both Cawti and Herth that I'd been killed? Herth so he'd leave me alone, Cawti so she'd kill Herth for me. I couldn't think of anything.

"*You know what your problem is, boss?*"

"Huh? Yeah. Everyone wants to tell me what my problem is."

"*Sorry I brought it up.*"

"Oh, go ahead."

"*You're trying to find a good trick to use, and you can't solve this with tricks.*"

That stopped me. I said, "*What you do mean?*"

"*Well, look, boss: What's been bothering you is that you're running into all these people who think you shouldn't be what you are, and you have to decide whether to change or not.*"

"Loiosh, what's bothering me is that there's an assassin out there who has my name and—"

"*Didn't you say yesterday that we'd been in worse places before?*"

146

"Yeah. And I've come up with some trick to get out of them."

"So why haven't you this time?"

"I'm too busy answering questions from jhereg who think that the only problem is great sorrow with my lot in life."

Loiosh giggled psionically and didn't say anything else. That's one trait Loiosh has that I've never found in anyone else: He knows when to stop pushing and let me just think about things. I suppose it comes from sharing my thoughts. I can't think of any other way to get it.

I teleported to the office. I wondered if my stomach would ever get used to the abuse. Cawti once told me that when she was working with Norathar they teleported almost everywhere, and her stomach never adjusted. They almost blew a job once, she said, because she threw up on the victim. I won't give you the details; she tells it better than I do.

I called Kragar into my office. "Well?"

"We've identified the assassin. His name is Quaysh."

"Quaysh? Unusual."

"It's Serioli. Means, 'He Who Designs Interesting Clasps For Ladies' Jewelry.'"

"I see. Do we have someone on him?"

"Yeah. A guy named Ishtvan. We used him once before."

"I remember. He was quick."

"That's the guy."

"Good. Who recognized Quaysh?"

"Sticks. They used to hang around together."

"Hmmm. Problem?"

"Not as far as I know. Business."

"Yeah. Okay, but tell Sticks to stay alert; if he knows that he knows who he is, and he doesn't know he knows—"

"What?"

"Just tell Sticks to be careful. Anything else important?"

"No. I'm putting together information on Herth's bodyguards, but it's going to be a while before we know enough to approach one."

I nodded and sent him about his business. I scratched under Loiosh's chin. I teleported—again—to South Adrilankha. I made my way to Kelly's place to see what was happening there. I stayed away from the corner I'd occupied before and took up a looser position down the street. Now the object was not to be noticed.

People who don't know this business seem to overrate the importance of looks in general and clothing in particular. This is because that's what one notices. You don't usually notice the way someone is walking, or the direction he's looking, or his movement through the crowd; you notice his appearance and his clothing. Nevertheless, that isn't what attracted your attention. You see people every day who look funny but don't attract attention. I mean, you certainly can't expect someone to say, "I didn't see this guy who looked funny," or, "There was someone wearing really weird clothes but I didn't notice him." An oddly shaped nose or unusual hair or a strange way of dressing are what you *remember* about someone you notice, but they aren't usually what calls him to your attention.

I was dressed oddly, for that area, but I was just being me, in the middle of the street where everyone else was, doing what everyone else was doing. No one noticed me, and I kept an eye on Kelly's flat to see if there was anything unusual going on. That is, I wanted to know if they'd discovered Franz.

After an hour or so I couldn't tell, so I made my way a little closer to the building, then a little closer, then I slipped around to the side, up against another one just like it. I pressed my ear against the wall. It was even thinner than I'd thought, so I had no trouble hearing what was going on inside.

They weren't talking about Franz at all.

Kelly was speaking, something about, "It's as if you're saying, 'I know you aren't interested, but—' under your breath." His voice was biting, sarcastic.

Cawti said something, but it was too low for me to

hear. Too low for Kelly, too, because he said, "Speak up," in a tone that made me wince. Cawti spoke again, and I still couldn't hear her, and then Paresh said, "That's absurd. It's twice as important now. You may not have noticed, but we're in the middle of an uprising. Every mistake we make now is twice as deadly. We can't afford *any* errors."

Then Cawti muttered something else and I heard several exclamations, and Gregory said, "If you feel that way, why did you join us in the first place?" Natalia said, "You're looking at it from *their* view. You've been trying to be an aristocrat all your life, and even now you're trying. But we aren't here to change places with them, and we aren't going to destroy them by accepting their lies as facts." And then Kelly said something, and others did as well, but I'm not going to relate any more of it. It isn't any of your business, and it isn't any of mine even though I heard it.

I listened, though, to quite a bit of it, getting redder and redder. Loiosh kept squeezing his talons on my shoulder and at one point said, *"Rocza's pretty upset."* I didn't answer because I didn't trust myself to speak, even to Loiosh. There was a door right around the corner from me, and I could have gone in there and Kelly would have died before he knew what hit him.

It was hard not to do it.

The only thing that distracted me was that I kept thinking things like, "How can she put up with that?" And, "Why does she *want* to put up with that?" It also occurred to me that all of the others were either very brave or very trusting. They knew as well as I did that Cawti could have killed the lot of them in seconds.

The woman I married would have done so, too.

I finally stole away from the building and had some klava.

She'd changed sometime in the last year, and I hadn't noticed. Maybe that was what bothered me the most. I mean, if I really loved her, wouldn't I have seen that she was turning from a walking death-machine into a . . . a whatever she was? But then, turn it around. I *did* love her; I could tell because it hurt so much, and I hadn't noticed, so there I was.

There was no point in wondering *why* she'd changed. No future in it, as Sticks would say. The question was, were we going to change together? No, let's be honest. The question was, was I going to pretend to be something I wasn't, or even try to *become* something I wasn't, in order to keep her? And when I put it that way I knew that I couldn't. I wasn't going to become another person on the chance that she'd come to love me again. She had married me, just as I was, and I had married her the same way. If she was going to turn away from me, I'd just have to live with it as best I could.

Or not. There was still Quaysh, who'd agreed to kill me, and Herth, who would try again if Quaysh failed. So maybe I wouldn't have to live with it at all. That would be convenient, but not really ideal. I ordered more klava, which came in a glass, which reminded me of Sheryl, which didn't cheer me up.

I was still in this gloomy frame of mind an hour later when Natalia came in accompanied by an Easterner I didn't know and a Teckla who wasn't Paresh. She saw me and nodded, then thought about it and joined me, after saying something to her companions. I invited her to sit and she did. I bought her a cup of tea because I was feeling expansive and because she didn't like klava. We just looked at each other until the tea arrived. It smelled better than the klava, and it came in a mug. I resolved to remember that.

Natalia's life was crudely sketched on her face. I mean, I couldn't see the details, but the outline was there. Her hair was dark but greying; the thin grey streaks that don't seem dignified but merely old. Her brow was wide and the furrows in it seemed permanent. There were deep lines next to her nose, which I'm sure had been a cute button when she was younger. Her face was thin and marked with tension, as if she went around with her jaw clenched. And yet, deep down behind it all, there was a sparkle in her eyes. She seemed to be in her early forties.

As she sipped on her tea and formed opinions of me that were as valid as mine of her, I said, "So, how did you get involved in all of this?"

She started to answer and I sensed that I was about to get a tract, so I said, "No, never mind. I'm not sure I want to hear."

She favored me with a sort of half-smile, which was the most cheerful thing I'd run into from her yet. She said, "You don't want to hear about my life as a harem girl for an Eastern king?"

I said, "Why yes, I would. I don't suppose you really were one though, were you?"

"I'm afraid not."

"Just as well," I said.

"I was a thief for a while, though."

"Yeah? Not a bad occupation. The hours are good, anyway."

"It's like anything else," she said. "It depends on your stature in the field."

I thought about Orcas who will knife anyone for twenty Imperials, and said, "I suppose. I take it you weren't at the top."

She nodded. "We lived on the other side of town." She meant the other side of South Adrilankha. To most Easterners, South Adrilankha was all of town there was. "That was," she continued, "after my mother died. My father would bring me into an inn and I would steal the coins the drinkers left on the bar, or sometimes cut their purses."

I said, "No, that isn't really the top of the profession, is it? But I suppose it's a living."

"After a fashion."

"Did you get caught?"

"Yes. Once. We'd agreed that if I was caught he'd go through the motions of beating me, as if it were my own idea. Then when I was finally caught, he did more than go through the motions."

"I see. Did you tell what really happened?"

"No. I was only about ten, and I was too busy crying and screaming that I'd never steal again, and I'm sorry, and anything else I could think of to say."

The waiter returned with more klava. I didn't touch it, having learned from experience.

I said, "Then what happened?"

She shrugged. "I never did steal again. We went into another inn, and I wouldn't steal anything, so my father took me out and beat me again. I ran away and I've never seen him since."

"You were how old, did you say?"

"Ten."

"Hmmm. How did you live, if you don't mind my asking?"

"Since all I knew about were inns, I went into one and asked to sweep the floor in exchange for a meal. The owner said yes, so that's what I did for a while. At first I was too scrawny to have any trouble with the customers, but later I had to hide during the evenings. I was charged for oil, so I'd sit in my room in the dark, covered with blankets. I didn't really mind, though. Having a room all to myself was so nice that I didn't miss the light or the heat.

"When the owner died I was twelve, and his widow sort of latched on to me. She stopped charging me for the oil, which was nice. But I guess the biggest thing she did for me was to teach me to read. From then on I spent all my time reading, mostly the same eight or nine books over and over again. I remember there was one that I couldn't understand no matter how many times I read it, and another one of fairy stories, and one was a play, something about a shipwreck. And one was all about where to grow what field crops for best results, or something. I even read that, which shows how desperate I was. I still didn't go down to the common room in the evening, and there wasn't anything else to do."

I said, "So there you were when Kelly came along, and he changed your life, and made you see this and that and the other, right?"

She smiled. "Something like that. I used to see him selling papers on the corner every day when I ran my errands. But one day, just out of nowhere, I realized that I could buy one and it would be something *new* to read. I had never heard of bookstores. I think Kelly was around twenty then.

"For the next year I'd buy a paper every week, then run off before he could talk to me. I had no idea what the paper was about, but I liked it. After a year or so, it finally began to sink in and I started thinking about what it was saying, and what it had to do with me. I remember it coming as a shock to me when I realized that there was something, somehow, *wrong* when a ten-year-old child had to go into inns to steal."

"That's true," I said. "A ten-year-old child should be able to steal in the streets."

"Stop it," she snapped, and I decided she probably had a point so I mumbled an apology and said, "So, anyway, that's when you decided to save the world."

I guess her years had taught her a certain kind of patience, because she didn't glare at me cynically as Paresh would have, or close up as Cawti would have. She shook her head and said, "It's never that simple. I started talking to Kelly, of course, and we started arguing. I didn't realize until later that the only reason I kept returning to him was that he was the only person I knew who listened to me and seemed to take me seriously. I don't think I ever would have done anything about it, but that was the year the tavern tax came down."

I nodded. That had been before my time, but I could still remember my father talking about it in that peculiar, hushed tone he always used when talking about something the Empire did that he didn't like. I said, "What happened then?"

She laughed. "A lot of things. The first thing was that the inn closed, almost right away. The owner sold it, probably for just enough to live on. The new owner closed it until the tax fuss settled, so I was out on the street without a job. That same day I saw Kelly, and his paper had a big article about it. I said something to him about his silly old paper, and this was *real*, and he tore into me like a dzur after lyorn. He said that was what the paper was about, and the only way to save the jobs was this and that and the other. I don't remember most of it, but I was pretty mad myself and not thinking too clearly. I told him the problem was the Empress was greedy, and he said that no, the Empress was desperate, because of this and that, and the next thing I knew he was sounding like he was on her side. I stormed off and didn't see him again for years.''

"What did you do?''

"I found another inn, this one on the Dragaeran side of town. Since Dragaerans can't tell how old we are anyway, and the owner thought I was 'cute,' they let me serve customers. It turned out that the last waiter had been killed in a knife fight the week before. I guess that should have told me what kind of place it was, and it was that kind of place, but I did all right. I found a flat just on this side of Twovine, and walked the two miles to work every day. The nice thing was that the walk took me past a little bookstore. I spent a lot of money there, but it was worth it. I especially loved history—Dragaeran, not human. And the stories, too. I guess I couldn't tell them apart very well. I used to pretend I was a Dzurlord, and I'd fight the battle of the Seven Pines then go charging up Dzur Mountain to fight the Enchantress all in one breath. What is it?''

I suppose I must have jumped a bit when she mentioned Dzur Mountain. I said, "Nothing. When did you meet Kelly again?''

My klava was cool enough to pick up and just barely warm enough to be worth drinking. I drank some. Natalia said, "It was after the head tax was instituted in the Eastern section. A couple who lived downstairs from me also knew how to read, and they ran into a group of people who were trying to get up a petition to the Empress against the tax.''

I nodded. Someone had come to my father's restaurant with a similar petition years later, even though we lived in the Dragaeran part of the city. My father had thrown him out. I said, "I've never understood why the head tax was even instituted. Was the Empire trying to keep Easterners out of the city?"

"It had to do largely with the uprisings in the eastern and northern duchies that ended forced labor. I've written a book on it. Would you like to buy a copy?"

"Never mind."

"Anyway," she continued, "my neighbors and I got involved with these people. We worked with them for a while, but I didn't like the idea of going to the Empire on our hands and knees. It seemed wrong. I guess my head was just filled with those histories and stories I'd read, and I was only fourteen, but it seemed to me that the only ones who ever got anything from the Empress had to ask boldly and prove themselves worthy." She said "boldly" and "worthy" with a bit of emphasis. "I thought we ought to do something wonderful for the Empire, then ask that the tax be lifted as our reward."

I smiled. "What did they say to that?"

"Oh, I never actually proposed it. I wanted to, but I was afraid they'd laugh at me." Her lips turned up briefly. "And of course they would have. But we had a few public meetings to talk about it, and Kelly started showing up at them, with, I think, four or five others. I don't remember what they said, but they made a big impression on me. They were younger than a lot of those there, but they seemed to know exactly what they were talking about, and they came in and left together, like a unit. They reminded me of the Dragon armies, I guess. So after one of the meetings I went up to Kelly and said, 'Remember me?' And he did, and we started talking, and we were arguing again inside of a minute, only this time I didn't walk away. I gave him my address and we agreed to stay in touch.

"I didn't join him for another year or so, after the riots, and the killings. It was just about the time the Empress finally lifted the head tax."

I nodded as if I knew the history she was speaking of. I said, "Was Kelly involved in that?"

"We were all involved. He wasn't behind the riots or anything, but he was there all the time. He was incarcerated for a while, at one of the camps they set up when they broke us up. I managed to avoid the Guards that time, though, even though I'd been around, too, when the Lumber Exchange was torched. That was what finally brought the troops in, you know. The Lumber Exchange was owned by a Dragaeran; an Iorich, I think."

"I hadn't known that," I said truthfully. "You've been with Kelly ever since?"

She nodded.

I thought about Cawti. "It must be difficult," I said. "I mean, he must be a hard man to work with."

"It's exciting. We're building the future."

I said, "Everyone builds the future. Everything we do every day builds the future."

"All right, I mean we're building it *consciously*. We know what we're doing."

"Yeah. Okay. You're building the future. To get it, you're sacrificing the present."

"What do you mean?" Her tone was genuinely inquisitive rather than snappy, which gave me some hope for her.

"I mean that you're so wrapped up in what you're doing that you're blind to the people around you. You're so involved in creating this vision of yours that you don't care how many innocent people are hurt." She started to speak but I kept going. "Look," I said, "we both know who I am and what I do, so there's no point pretending otherwise, and if you think it's inherently evil, then there isn't anything more to say. But I can tell you that I have never, *never* intentionally hurt an innocent person. And I'm including Dragaerans as people, so don't think I'm pulling one on you that way because I'm not."

She caught my eye and held it. "I didn't think you were. And I won't even discuss what you mean by innocent. All I can say is that if you really believe what you've just said, nothing I can say will change your mind, so there isn't any point in discussing it.''

I relaxed, not realizing that I'd been tense. I guess I'd expected her to lambaste me or something. I suddenly wondered why I cared, and decided that Natalia seemed to be the most reasonable of these people that I'd yet met, and I somehow wanted to like, and be liked by, at least one of them. That was stupid. I'd given up trying to make people "like" me when I was twelve years old, and had the results of that attitude beaten into me in ways I'll never forget.

And with that thought a certain anger came, and with the anger a certain strength. I kept it off my face, but it came back to me then, as a chilly, refreshing wave. I had started down the path that led me to this point many, many years before, and I had taken those first steps because I hated Dragaerans. That was my reason then, it was my reason now, it was enough.

Kelly's people did everything for ideals I could never understand. To them, people were "the masses," individuals only mattered by what they did for the movement. Such people could never love. Not purely, unselfishly, with no thought for why and how and what it would do. And, similarly, they could never hate; they were too wrapped up in *why* someone did something to be able to hate him for doing it.

But I hated. I could feel my hatred inside of me, spinning like a ball of ice. Most of all, right now, I hated Herth. No, I didn't really *want* to hire someone to send him for a walk, I wanted to do it myself. I wanted to feel that tug of a body as it jerks and kicks while I hold the handle and the life erupts from it like water from the cold springs of the Eastern Mountains. That's what I wanted, and what you want makes you who you are.

I put down a few coins to pay for the klava and the tea. I don't know how much Natalia knew of what was going on in my head, but she knew I was done talking. She thanked me and we stood up at the same time. I bowed and thanked her for her company.

As I walked out, she picked up her two companions by sight and they left the place just ahead of me, turned, and waited for her by the door. As I left, the Easterner looked at my grey cloak with the stylized jhereg on it and sneered. If the Teckla had done it I'd have killed him, but it was the Easterner so I just kept walking.

13-

. . .remove cat hairs. . .

The chimes sounded, light and tinkling, as I stepped
into the shop. My grandfather was writing in a bound
tablet with an old-fashioned pencil. As I came in he
looked up and smiled.

"Vladimir!"

"Hello, Noish-pa." I hugged him. We sat down and
he said hello to Loiosh. Ambrus jumped into my lap
and I greeted him properly. Ambrus never purred when
stroked, but he somehow let you know when he liked
what you were doing anyway. My grandfather told me
once that Ambrus only purred when they were working
magic together; the purr was a sign that everything was
all right.

I studied my grandfather. Was he looking a bit older,
a little more worn than he used to? I wasn't sure. It's
hard to look at a familiar face as if it were that of a
stranger. For some reason my eyes were drawn to his
ankles, and I noticed how thin and frail they looked,
even for his size. Yet, again for his size, his chest seemed
large and well-muscled beneath a faded tunic of red and
green. His head, bald save for the thinnest fringe of
white hair, gleamed in the candlelight.

"So," he said after a while.

"How are you feeling?"

"I am fine, Vladimir. And you?"

"About the same, Noish-pa."

"Yes. There is something on your mind?"

I sighed. "Were you around in two twenty-one?"

He raised his eyebrows. "The riots? Yes. That was a bad time." He shook his head as he spoke and the corners of his mouth fell. But it was funny; it seemed, at the same time, that his eyes lit up just a bit, way down deep.

I said, "You were involved?"

"Involved? How could I not be involved? It was everyone; we were part of it or we hid from it, but we were all involved."

"Was my father involved?"

He gave me a look that I couldn't read. Then he said, "Yes, your father, he was there. He and I, and your grandmother too, and my brother Jani. We were at Twovine and Hilltop when the Empire tried to break us." His voice hardened a bit as he said that. "Your father killed a Guard, too. With a butcher knife."

"He did?"

He nodded.

I didn't say anything for a while, trying to see how I felt about this. It seemed odd, and I wished I'd known it while my father was still alive. There was a brief pang from knowing that I'd never see him again. I finally said, "And you?"

"Oh, they gave me a post after the fight, so I guess I was there too."

"A post?"

"I was a block delegate, for M'Gary Street north of Elm. So when we met, I had to go there for everyone from our neighborhood and say what we wanted."

"I hadn't known about that. Dad never talked about it."

"Well, he was unhappy. That was when I lost your grandmother—when they came back in."

"The Empire?"

"Yes. They came back with more troops—Dragons

who had fought in the East.''

"Would you like to tell me about it?''

He sighed and looked away for a moment. I guess he was thinking about my grandmother. I wished I'd met her. "Perhaps another time, Vladimir.''

"Sure. All right. I noticed that Kelly looked at you as if he recognized you. Was it from then?''

"Yes. I knew him. He was young then. When we spoke of him before I didn't know it was the same Kelly.''

"Is he a good man, Noish-pa?''

He glanced at me quickly. "Why this question?''

"Because of Cawti, I suppose.''

"Hmmph. Well, yes, he is good, perhaps, if what he does you call good.''

I tried to decipher that, then came at it from another angle. "You didn't seem to think much of Cawti being involved with these people. Why is that, if you were involved in it yourself?''

He spread his hands. "Vladimir, if there is an uprising against the landlords, then of course you want to help. What else can you do? But this is different. She is looking to make trouble where there is none. And it was never something that came between Ibronka—your grandmother—and me.''

"It didn't?''

"Of course not. That happened, and we were all a part of it. We had to be part of it or we would be with the counts and the landlords and the bankers. It was one or the other then, it was not a thing for which I abandoned my family.''

"I see. Is that what you want to tell Cawti, if she comes to see you?''

"If she asks I will tell her.''

I nodded. I wondered how Cawti would react, and decided that I no longer knew her well enough to guess. I changed the topic then, but I kept noticing that he gave me funny looks from time to time. Well, I could hardly blame him.

I let things churn around in my head. Franz's ghost or

no Franz's ghost, it would be most convenient for me if Kelly and his whole band were to fall off the edge of the world, but there was no good way to arrange that.

It also seemed that the biggest problem with getting to Herth was that he could take as much time as he wanted in getting me, and it wasn't hurting him at all. The Easterners had cut back on his business in some neighborhoods, but not all, and he still had his contacts and hired muscle and legmen all set to go back to business as usual as soon as the time was right. And he was a Dragaeran; he would live another thousand years or so, so what was his hurry?

If I could make him move at all, I might be able to force him out into the open, where I could get another shot at him. Furthermore . . . hmmm. My grandfather was silent, watching me as if he knew how fast my brain was working. I started putting together a new plan. Loiosh had no comment on it. I looked at it from a couple of different directions as I sipped herb tea. I held the plan in my head and bounced it off several different possible problems, and it rebounded just fine. I decided to go ahead with it.

"You have an idea, Vladimir?"

"Yes, Noish-pa."

"Well, you should be about it then."

I stood up. "You're right."

He nodded and said nothing more. I bade him goodbye while Loiosh flew out of the door in front of me. Loiosh said everything was all right. I was still feeling worried about Quaysh. It would be much harder to implement my plan if I were dead.

I had only walked a couple of blocks when I was approached. I was passing an outdoor market, and she was leaning against a building, her hands behind her back. She seemed to be about fifteen years old and wore a peasant skirt of yellow and blue. The skirt was slit, which meant nothing, but her legs were shaved, which meant a great deal.

She moved away from the wall as I walked by and she said hello. I stopped and wished her a pleasant day. It suddenly occurred to me that this could be a set-up; I ran a hand through my hair and adjusted my cloak. She seemed to think I was trying to impress her and showed me a pair of dimples. I wondered how much extra the dimples were worth.

"Anything, Loiosh?"

"Too crowded to tell for sure, boss, but I don't see Quaysh."

I decided it was probably just what it seemed to be.

She asked if I cared to take her somewhere for a drink. I said maybe. She asked if I cared to take her somewhere for a screw. I asked her how much, she said ten and seven, which worked out to an Imperial, which was a third of what my tags were charging.

I said, "Sure." She nodded without bothering with the dimples and led me around the corner. I let a knife fall into my hand, just in case. We entered an inn that displayed a sign with several bees buzzing about a hive. She spoke to the innkeeper and I put my knife away. I handed him seven silver coins. He gestured with his head toward the stairs and said, "Room three." The inn was pretty full for the afternoon, and there was a haze of blue smoke. It smelled old and foul and stale. I would have guessed that everyone in the place was a drunk.

She led me up to room three. I insisted she go in first and watched her for signs that someone else was in there. I didn't see any. When she turned back to me, Loiosh flew in.

"Okay, boss. It's safe."

She said, "Do you want *that* in here, too?"

I said, "Yeah."

She shrugged and said, "Okay."

I entered the room. The curtain fell shut behind me. There was a mattress on the floor and a table next to it. I gave her an Imperial. "Keep it," I said.

"Thanks."

She took off her blouse. Her body was young. I didn't move. She looked at me and said, "Well?"

As I came toward her, she put on a fake dreamy smile, turned her face up to me, and held her arms out.

I slapped her. She stepped back and said, "Hey!" I moved in and slapped her again. She said, "None of that!" I drew a knife from my cloak and held it up. She screamed.

As the sound echoed and bounced around the room, I grabbed her arm and dragged her into a corner next to the doorway and held her there. There was fear in her eyes now. I said, "That's enough. Open your mouth again and I'll kill you." She nodded, watching my face. I heard footsteps outside and I let go of her. The curtain swung aside and a big bludgeon entered, followed by a large Easterner with a black beard.

He charged in, stopped when he saw the empty room, and started to look around. Before he had a chance to do so I had grabbed hold of his hair and was pulling his head into my knife, which was pressed against the back of his neck. I said, "Drop the club." He tensed as if he were about to spring and I pressed harder. He relaxed and the club fell to the floor. I turned to the whore. The look on her face told me that this was her pimp, rather than just a bouncer for the inn or some interested citizen. "Okay," I told her. "Get out of here."

She ran around us to pick up her blouse and left without looking at either of us, or stopping to dress. The pimp said, "You a bird?"

I blinked. "Bird? Phoenix. Phoenix Guard. I like that. Lord Khaavren will like that. No, I'm not. Don't be stupid. Who do you work for?"

He said, "Huh?"

I kicked the back of his knee and he sat down. I knelt on his chest and put the point of my knife in front of his left eye. I repeated my question. He said, "I don't work for anyone. I'm on my own."

I said, "So I can do whatever I want to you, and no one will protect you, is that right?"

This put a different light on things. He said, "No, I got protection."

I said, "Good. Who?"

Then his eyes fell on the jhereg emblazoned on my

cloak. He licked his lips and said, "I don't want to get involved."

I couldn't help smiling at that. "How much more involved can you get?"

"Yeah, but—"

I created some pain for him. He yelped. I said, "Who protects you?"

He gave me an Eastern name that I didn't recognize. I moved the knife a bit away from his face, relaxed my hold on him a little and said, "Okay. I'm working for Kelly. Know who I mean?" He nodded. I said, "Good. I want you off the streets. For good. You're out of business as of now, okay?" He nodded again. I grabbed a lock of his hair then, sliced it off with my knife, held it in front of him and put it away inside my cloak. His eyes widened. I said, "I can find you now any time I want to. Understand?" He understood. "All right. I'm going to be back here in a few days. I'll want to see that fine young lady I just spoke to. And I want to see that she hasn't been hurt. If she has been I'll take pieces of you home with me. If I can't find her, I won't bother with the pieces. Can you understand that?" Apparently we were still communicating; he nodded. I said, "Good," and left him there. I saw no sign of the tag.

I left the inn and walked west about half a mile and went into a little cellar place. I asked the host, an ugly, squinty guy, if he knew where I could find some action.

"Action?"

"Action. You know, shereba, s'yang-stones, whatever."

He looked at me blankly until I passed an Imperial across the counter. Then he gave me an address a few doors down. I followed his directions and, sure enough, there were three shereba tables in use. I spotted the guy who was running it, sitting with the back of his chair against a wall, dozing. I said, "Hi. Sorry to bother you."

He opened one eye. "Yeah?"

I said, "Know who Kelly is?"

"Huh?"

"Kelly. You know, the guy who shut down the whole—"

"Yeah, yeah. What about him?"

"I work for him."

"Huh?"

"You're out of business. Game over. Closed. Get everyone out of here."

The room was small, and I'd been making no effort to keep my voice down. The card playing had stopped and everyone was watching me. Just as the pimp had, this guy noticed the stylized jhereg on my cloak. He seemed puzzled. "Look," he said. "I don't know who you are, or what kind of game you're playing—"

I stole a trick from the Phoenix Guards: I smacked him across the side of his head with the hilt of a dagger, then brandished the dagger. I said, "Does this straighten things out for you?" I heard movement behind me.

"Trouble, Loiosh?"

"No, boss. They're leaving."

"Good."

When the room was empty, I let the guy up. I said, "I'll be checking on you. If this place does any more business, I'll have your ass. Now get out."

He left in a hurry. I left more slowly. I allowed myself one evil chuckle, just because I felt like it. By the time I was done it was early evening and I'd terrorized three whores, as many pimps, two game operators, a bookie and a cleaner.

A good day's work, I decided. I headed back to the office to talk to Kragar, to put the second part of the plan into operation.

Kragar thought I was crazy.

"You're crazy, Vlad."

"Probably."

"They'll all just desert you."

"I'm going to keep paying them."

"How?"

"I'm rich, remember?"

"How long can that last?"

"A few weeks, of which I'll only need one."

"One?"

"Yeah. I spent today stirring up Herth and Kelly and pointing them at each other." I gave him a quick summary of the day's activities. "It'll take them maybe a day, each, to figure out who really did it. Herth will come after me with everything he has, and Kelly. . . ."

"Yeah?"

"Wait and see."

He sighed. "All right. You want every business you own shut down by tomorrow morning. Fine. Everyone in hiding for a week. Fine. You say you can afford it, okay. But this other business, in South Adrilankha, I just can't see it."

"What's to see? We're just continuing what I started today."

"But fires? Explosions? That's no way to—"

"We have people who can do that sort of thing properly, Kragar. We were trained by Laris, remember?"

"Sure, but the Empire—"

"Exactly."

"I don't get it."

"You don't have to. Just handle the details."

"Okay, Vlad. It's your show. What about our own places? Like this one, for instance."

"Yeah. Get hold of the Bitch Patrol and protect them. Full sorcerous protection, including teleport blocks, and increase what we have here. I can—"

"—Afford it. Yeah, I know. I still think you're crazy."

"So will Herth. But he's going to have to deal with it anyway."

"He'll come after you, if that's what you want."

"Yep."

He sighed, shook his head and left. I leaned back in my chair, feet up on my desk, and made sure I hadn't missed anything.

●　　●　　●

Cawti was home when I got there. We said hello and how was your day and like that. We settled down in the living room, next to each other on the couch so we could feel nothing had changed, but a foot or so apart so we didn't have to take chances. I got up first, stretching, and announcing that I was going to go to sleep. She hoped I'd sleep well. I suggested that she probably needed some sleep herself, and she allowed that she did and would be in soon. I retired. Loiosh and Rocza were a bit subdued. I can't imagine why. I fell asleep quickly, as I always do when I have a plan working. It's one of the things that keeps me sane.

I teleported to the office early the next morning and waited for reports. Herth was about as quick on the up-take as I'd thought he'd be. I heard that attempts had been made to penetrate the spells around my office building and one or two other places.

"Glad you suggested we protect them, Kragar," I said.

He mumbled.

"Something bothering you, Kragar?"

He said, "Heh. I hope you know what you're doing."

I started to say, "I always know what I'm doing," but that would have rung a bit hollow, so I said, "I think so." That seemed to satisfy him.

"Okay, then, what's next?"

I mentioned someone important in the organization, and what my next step was. Kragar looked startled, then nodded. "Sure," he said, "He owes you one, doesn't he?"

"Or two or three. Set it up for today if possible."

"Right."

He was back in an hour. "The Blue Flame," he said. We shared a smile of common memories. "The eighth hour. He said he'd take care of all protection, which means he knows something of what's going on."

I nodded. "He would."

"Do you trust him?"

"Yeah," I said. "I'll have to trust him eventually, so

I might as well trust him for this."

Kragar nodded.

Later in the day I received word that we'd torched a couple of buildings in South Adrilankha. By now Herth must be biting his nails, wishing he could get his hands on me. I chuckled. *Soon*, I told him, *soon*.

I felt a funny sort of mental itch, and knew what it meant.

"Who is it?"

"*Chimov. I'm near Kelly's headquarters.*"

"What's up?"

"*They're moving out of the place.*"

"Ah ha. Find out where they're going."

"*Will do. They have a whole crowd. It looks like they expect trouble. They're also posting handbills, and passing out leaflets all over the place.*"

"Have you read one?"

"*Yeah. It's about a mass meeting for tomorrow afternoon in Naymat Park. The big print at the top says 'A Call To Arms.'*"

"Well," I said. "Excellent. Stay with it, and keep out of trouble."

"*Right, boss.*"

"Kragar!"

"Yeah?"

"Oh. Get someone over to Kelly's headquarters. Make it four or five. As soon as it's empty, go in and trash the place. Break up any furniture that's left, smash up walls, wreck the kitchen, that kind of thing."

"Okay."

I spent the rest of the day like that. Messages would come in, about this or that work of destruction completed, or some attack by Herth foiled, and I'd sit there and snap out the response to it. I was operating efficiently again, and it felt so good I kept going far into the evening, tightening this or that piece of surveillance, adding this or that nudge to Kelly or Herth. Of course, the office was just about the safest place for me to be just then, which was another good reason for working late.

As evening wore on, I exchanged messages with an Organization contact inside the Imperial Palace, and learned that, yes, the powers-that-be had noted what was going on in South Adrilankha. Herth's name had come up, but so far mine had not. Perfect.

When it got near to the eighth hour after noon I collected Sticks, Glowbug, Smiley and Chimov and we made our way to the Blue Flame. I left them near the door, because my guest had already arrived and he had promised to handle protection. And, in fact, I noticed a pair of customers and three waiters who looked like enforcers. I bowed as I approached the table.

He said, "Good evening, Vlad."

I said, "Good evening, Demon. Thanks for coming." He nodded and I sat. The Demon, for those of you who don't know, was a big man on the Jhereg council—the group that makes decisions affecting the whole business end of House Jhereg. He was generally considered the number-two man in the Organization; not someone to mess around with. However, as Kragar had mentioned, he owed me a favor for some "work" I'd done for him recently.

We exchanged amenities for a while, then, as the food showed up, he said, "So, you've gotten yourself into trouble, I hear."

"A bit," I said. "Nothing I can't handle, though."

"Indeed? Well, that's nice to hear." He gave me a kind of puzzled look. "Then why did you want to meet with me?"

"I'd like to arrange for nothing to happen."

He blinked. "Go on," he said.

"The Empire may start to take notice of the game that Herth and I are playing, and when the Empire notices, the Council notices."

"I see. And you want us not to interfere."

"Right. Can you give me a week to settle things?"

"Can you keep the trouble confined to South Adrilankha?"

"Pretty much," I said. "I won't be touching him anywhere else, and I've shut down and protected everything I own, so it will be hard for him to hit me. There may be one or two bodies turning up, but nothing to cause great excitement."

"The Empire isn't too keen on bodies turning up, Vlad."

"There shouldn't be too many. None, in fact, if my people are careful. And, as I say, it ought to be settled in a week."

He studied me. "You have something going, don't you?"

I said, "Yeah."

He smiled and shook his head. "No one can say you aren't resourceful, Vlad. All right, you have a week. I'll take care of it."

I said, "Thanks."

He offered to pay for the meal, but I insisted. It was my pleasure.

14-

. . .brush, removing white particles. . .

I got the full escort home from my bodyguards. They
left me just outside the door, and as I stepped past the
threshold I felt the draining of a tension that I hadn't
known had been building up. You see, while my office is
very well protected, one's home is strictly inviolate by
Jhereg custom. Why? I don't know. Perhaps for the
same reason temples are; just a matter of you ought to
be safe somewhere no matter what, and everyone is too
open to attacks this way. Maybe there's another reason
for it. I'm not sure. But I've never heard of this custom
being violated.

Of course, I'd never heard of anyone stealing from
the Jhereg before it happened, either, but you have to
depend on something.

Don't you?

Anyway, I was home and safe and Cawti was in the
living room, reading her tabloid. My heart skipped, but
I recovered and smiled. "Home early," I remarked.

She didn't smile when she looked up at me. "You
bastard," she said, and there was real feeling behind the
words. I felt my face flushing, and a sick feeling started
in the pit of my stomach and spread out to all salient

points. It wasn't as if I hadn't known she'd find out what I was doing, or hadn't known what her reaction was going to be, so why should it come as such a shock when she did just what I'd expected her to?

I swallowed and said, "Cawti—"

"Didn't you think I'd find out what you were up to, beating up Herth's people and blaming it on us?"

"No, I knew you would."

"Well?"

"I'm working a plan."

"A plan," she said, her voice dripping contempt.

"I'm doing what I have to."

She managed an expression that was half-sneer and half-scowl. "What you have to," she said, as if she were discussing the mating habits of teckla.

"Yeah," I said.

"You have to do everything you can to destroy the only people who—"

"The only people who are going to cost you your life? Yes. And for what?"

"A better life for—"

"Oh, stop it. Those people are so full of great ideals that they can't manage to understand that there are *people* in the world, people who shouldn't get tromped over without reason. *Individuals.* Starting with you and me. Here we are, on the verge of—I don't know what— on account of these great saviors of humanity, and all you can see is what's happening to *them*. You're blind to what's happening to us. Or else you don't care anymore. And this doesn't tell you that there's something wrong with them?"

She laughed, and it was a hateful laugh. "Something wrong with *them*? That's your conclusion? Something wrong with the movement?"

"Yeah," I said. "That's my conclusion."

Her mouth twisted, she said, "Do you expect me to buy that?"

I said, "What do you mean, buy?"

"I mean, you can't sell that product."

"What am I supposed to be selling?"

"You can sell anything you want, as far as I'm concerned."

"Cawti, you aren't making sense. What—"

"Just shut up," she said. "Bastard."

She'd never called me names before. It's still funny, how that stung.

For the first time in quite a while I felt anger toward her. I stood there looking at her, feeling my feet seem to attach to the floor and my face harden, and I welcomed the cold rush of it, at first. She stood there, glaring at me (I hadn't even noticed her standing up) and that just fed into it. There was a ringing in my ears, and it came to me, as from a distance, that I was out of control again.

I took a step toward her, and her eyes grew wide and she backed up half a step. I don't know what would have happened if she hadn't, but that was sufficient to give me enough control to turn and leave the house.

"Boss, no! Not outside!"

I didn't answer him. In fact, his words didn't even penetrate until the cool evening breeze hit my face. Then I understood that I was in some sort of danger. I thought of teleporting to Castle Black, but I also knew that I was in no state of mind to teleport. On the other hand, if I were attacked, that would suit my mood perfectly.

I started walking, keeping as tight a control on myself as I could, which wasn't very. Then I remembered the last time I'd gone charging around the city with no regard for who saw me, and that sent chills through me, which cooled me down a bit and I became more careful.

A little more careful.

But I have to think that Verra, my Demon-Goddess, watched over me that night. Herth had to have had Quaysh and everyone else looking for me, yet I wasn't attacked. I stormed through my area, looking at all the closed shops, at my office with yet a few lights burning, at the dead fountain in Malak Circle, and I wasn't even threatened. While I was in Malak Circle I stopped for a while, sitting at the edge of the crumbling fountain. Loiosh looked around anxiously, anticipating an attack, yet it felt as if what he was doing had nothing to do with me.

As I sat there, faces began to appear before me. Cawti looked at me with pity on her face, as if I had caught the plague and wouldn't recover. My grandfather looked stern but loving. An old friend named Nielar stared at me, calmly. And Franz appeared, oddly enough. He gave me a look of accusation. That was funny. Why should I care about *him* of all people? I mean, I hadn't known him at all while he was alive, and the little bit I'd known of him after his death told me that we had nothing in common. Except for the unique circumstances of our meeting, he would have had nothing whatever to do with me.

Why did my subconscious decide to bring him up?

I knew plenty of Dragaerans who seemed to feel that the Teckla were Teckla because that was how things were, and whatever happened to them was fine, and if they wanted to better themselves, let them. These were the lords of the land, and they enjoyed being what they were, and they deserved it and no one else did, and that was that. Okay. I could understand that attitude. It had nothing to do with the way things really were for the Teckla, but it made a lot of sense for the way things were for the Dragons.

I knew a few Dragaerans who cried aloud over the plight of the Teckla, and the Easterners for that matter, and gave money to charities for the poor and the homeless. Most of them were fairly well-off, and sometimes I wondered at my own contempt for them. But I always had the feeling that they secretly despised those they helped, and were so guilt-ridden that they blinded themselves to the way things were in order to convince themselves that they were doing some good, that they actually made a difference.

And then there were Kelly and his people; so wrapped up in how they would save a world that they didn't care about anyone or anything except the little ideas they had floating around their little heads. Completely, utterly ruthless, all in the name of humanity.

Those were the three groups I saw around me, and it came to me then, as I imagined Franz looking at me with an expression that oozed sincerity as a festering wound oozes pus, that I had to decide where I fit.

Well, I certainly wasn't with the third group. I could only kill individuals, not whole societies. I have a high opinion of my own abilities, but it isn't so high that I'm willing to destroy an entire society on the strength of an opinion, nor would I be willing to set up thousands of people to be slaughtered if I was wrong. When someone messed up my life—as had happened before and would happen again—I took it personally. I wasn't ready to blame it on something as nebulous as a society and try to arouse the population to destroy it for me. I took it as it was; someone messing up my life, to be dealt with using a clean, simple dagger. No, I wasn't about to find myself with Kelly's people.

The second group? No; I had earned what I had, and no one was going to make me feel guilty about having it, not even the Franz that my subconscious dredged up in a futile effort to torment me. Those who wallowed in guilt they hadn't earned deserve no better than they gave themselves.

I had once been part of the first group, and perhaps I still was, but now I didn't like the idea. *They* were the people I had hated so long. Not Dragaerans, but those who lorded it over the rest of us, and displayed their wealth, culture and education like a club they could beat us with. *They* were my enemies, even if I'd spent most of my life unaware of it. *They* were the ones I wanted to show that I could come up out of nowhere and make something of myself. And how surprised they had been when I did so!

Yet I couldn't, even now, consider myself one of them. Maybe I was, but I couldn't make myself believe it. Only once in my life have I truly hated myself, and that was when Herth broke me and made me face the fact that there was more to life than the will to succeed;

that sometimes, no matter how hard he tries, there are things a man *can't* succeed at, because the forces around him are stronger than he is. That was the only time I'd hated myself. To put myself into the first group would be to hate myself again, and I couldn't do that.

So, where did that leave me? Everywhere and nowhere. On the outside, looking in. Unable to help, unable to hinder; a commentator on the theatrics of life.

Did I believe that? I wondered, but no answer came forth. On the other hand, I was certainly having an effect on Kelly. Herth, too, for that matter. That might have to be enough for me. I noticed that the air had become chilly, and I realized that I was calmer now and that I should go somewhere safe.

Since I was already at Malak Circle, I stopped in at the office and said hello to a few people who were still working. Melestav was in. I said, "Don't you ever go home?"

"Yeah, well, things are popping right now, and if I don't keep things organized these bozos will screw everything up."

"Herth is still trying to get us?"

"Here and there. The big news is that the Empire has moved into South Adrilankha."

"What?"

"About an hour ago, a whole Company of Phoenix Guards came in and just occupied the place as if it were an Eastern city."

I stared at him. "Was anyone hurt?"

"A few score of Easterners were killed or injured, I guess."

"Kelly?"

"No, none of his people were hurt. They moved, remember."

"That's right. What reason did the Empire give?"

"Disturbances, that kind of thing. Isn't this what you were expecting?"

"Not this quickly, or in that much force, or with anyone killed."

"Yeah, well you know Phoenix Guards. They hate

dealing with Easterners anyway.''

"Yeah. Do you have Kelly's new address?''

He nodded and scribbled it out on a piece of paper. I glanced at it and saw that I could find the place; it was only a few blocks from the old one.

"Oh, by the way,'' said Melestav, "Sticks wants to see you. He was thinking tomorrow, but he's still hanging around in case you came in this evening. Should I get him?''

"Oh, all right. Send him in.''

I wandered into my office and sat down. A few minutes later Sticks showed up. He said, "Can I talk to you for a minute?''

I said, "Sure.''

He said, "You know Bajinok?''

I said, "Yeah.''

"He wanted me to help set you up. You said you like to know about these things.''

I nodded. "I do. Okay, you got a bonus coming.''

"Thanks.''

"When did he talk to you?''

"About an hour ago.''

"Where?''

"The Flame.''

"Who was with you?''

"No one.''

"Okay. Be careful.''

Sticks mumbled something and walked out. I blinked. Was I beyond being shocked or frightened? Or was I too far gone to care? No, I cared. I hoped nothing would happen to him. He'd also been the one to identify Quaysh, and between the two things that could make him a real juicy target.

In fact, an irresistible target.

And why would they wait? An hour ago, he said? This wasn't an especially difficult piece of work, and Herth had people on his payroll who did the simple cutthroat things because it was part of their jobs.

I stood up. "Melestav!''

"Yeah, boss?''

"Has Sticks left?"

"I think so."

I cursed and sprinted through the building after him. A little voice in my head said, "Set-up," and I wondered. I opened the door and Loiosh flew out ahead of me. I stepped out onto the street, and looked around.

Well, yes and no.

I mean, it *was* a set-up, but I wasn't the one being set up. I saw Sticks, and I saw the form coming quickly up behind him. I yelled, "Sticks!" and he turned and stepped to the side as a shadowy figure lurched toward him and stumbled. There was a dull thud as Sticks nailed the assassin with a club, and the latter fell to the ground. It was only then that I realized I'd thrown a knife. I came up to them.

Sticks retrieved my knife from the back of the individual on the ground before us, wiped it on the fellow's cloak, and handed it to me. I caused it to vanish. "Did you shine him?"

Sticks shook his head. "He'll be all right, I think, if he wakes up before he bleeds to death. Should we get him off the street?"

"No. Leave him here. I'll have Melestav let Bajinok know he's here, and they can do their own clean-up."

"Okay. Thanks."

"Don't mention it. Be careful, all right?"

"All right." He shook his head. "I sometimes wonder why I'm in this business."

"Yeah," I said. "Me, too."

I went back inside and gave Melestav the necessary orders. He didn't seem surprised, but then I haven't surprised him since the time I brought Kiera the Thief into the office.

I sat down at my desk again and pushed aside all thoughts of what the Phoenix Guards were doing in South Adrilankha, and my responsibility for it. It wasn't that I didn't care, but I was involved in a war right now, and if I kept letting myself be distracted I was going to make a mistake, and after that I wouldn't be able to save Cawti, Sticks, myself or anyone else.

I had a war to win.

Sometime before, I'd been involved in a war where I was one of the contestants, as opposed to a mere participant. I learned the importance of information, of striking first, of keeping your enemy off balance and of thoroughly protecting your own area and people.

Herth had a bigger organization than I, but since I was the one who made it a full-scale war, I'd gotten in some good strikes at him. Furthermore, I had pretty much made sure that he couldn't hurt my organization. Of course, doing this resulted in a drastic loss of income, but I was quite well off at the moment, and I didn't think this would take long. I didn't really intend or expect to win this war in the usual way, I just wanted to force Herth out into the open so I could kill him. I thought to do it by making such a mess in his area that he'd have to take a hand in keeping it together.

That was half the plan, at any rate. The half involving Kelly was harder, but I had hopes for it. Damn Phoenix Guards, I thought. Damn the Empress. Damn Lord Khaavren. But Kelly was still in the same mess. I mean, what other choice did he have, if everyone else behaved as expected? And he probably realized that, judging from Cawti's reaction—

I thought about Cawti, and my plans and schemes fell away from my fingertips, where they'd been dancing for me. I saw only her for a moment and I cursed under my breath.

"So talk to her, boss."

"I just tried that, remember?"

"No, you argued with her. What if you tell her your whole plan?"

"She won't like it."

"But she might not be as upset with you as she is now."

"I doubt it will matter."

"Boss, you remember that what first got you upset was that she hadn't told you that she was involved with Kelly and those people?"

"Yeah . . . okay."

I sat for a bit longer, then went over to the front door, waving away bodyguards. I took a deep breath, made sure my mind was clear, drew on the Orb, shaped the threads of power, twisted them around myself and pulled them tight. There was the awful lurch, and I stood in the entry way outside the door to my flat. I leaned against the wall until the nausea was under control.

The instant I walked into the flat I knew something was wrong. So did Loiosh. I stood just inside the door, not closing it, and let a knife fall into my right hand. I looked carefully around the living room, trying to determine what was funny. And you know, we didn't get it? After fully ten minutes, we just gave up and went inside, still being careful, Loiosh going in ahead of me.

No, no one was waiting to kill me.

No one was waiting for me at all. I went into the bedroom, and saw that Cawti's clothing had been cleared out of the closet. I went back into the living room and saw that, of all things, the *lant* was missing, which is what Loiosh and I had noticed when we first came in. Funny how things like that work.

I tried to reach Cawti psionically but I couldn't. She wasn't interested in receiving my communication, or else I wasn't concentrating well enough to reach her. Yes, I decided, that must be it, I just couldn't think clearly enough right now to communicate psionically.

"Kragar?"

"Yes, Vlad?"

"Any word from Ishtvan?"

"Not yet."

"Okay. That's all."

Yeah, that must be the problem.

I went into the bedroom and shut the door before Loiosh could enter. I lay down on the bed—on Cawti's side—and tried to bring tears. I couldn't. At last, fully dressed, I slept.

15-

. . .remove honing-oil stains. . .

I woke up very early in the morning feeling tired and still dirty. I undressed, bathed, and climbed back into bed and slept a bit longer.

It was only when I woke up the second time, just before noon, that I remembered that Cawti had left. I allowed myself to stare at the ceiling for two minutes, then forced myself to get up. I kept stopping as I shaved, looking to see if there was any outward change in the face that stared back at me. I didn't see anything.

"Well, boss?"

"I'm glad you're around, chum."

"Know what you're going to do?"

"You mean about Cawti?"

"Yeah."

"Not really. I didn't know she'd leave. Or I didn't believe it. Or I didn't know how hard it would hit me. I feel like I'm dead inside, you know what I mean?"

"I can feel it, boss. That's why I asked."

"I don't know if I'm up to handling what's going to happen now."

"You need to have things settled with Cawti."

"I know. Maybe I should try to find her."

"You'll have to be careful. Herth—"

"Yeah."

I made myself ready, checked my hardware and teleported to South Adrilankha. I rested a while in a small
park, with a good view all around me—a very bad place
for Quaysh—then I headed for an eating place. On the
way I spotted and avoided two groups of Phoenix
Guards. I found a table and ordered klava. As the
waiter was leaving I said, "Excuse me."

"Yes, my lord?"

"Would you please bring that in a cup?"

He didn't even look startled. "Yes, my lord," he
said. Just like that. And he did it. All this time, and the
solution was as easy as asking for it. Wasn't that pro-
found?

"I doubt it, boss."

*"Me, too, Loiosh. But it starts the day right. And
speaking of starting the day, can you find Rocza?"*

A moment later Loiosh said in a hurt tone, *"No.
She's blocking me."*

"I didn't know she could do that."

"Neither did I. Why would she?"

*"Because Cawti figured out that I could trace her that
way. Damn. Well, okay, so we go to Kelly's place and
either wait for her or make them tell us where she is.
Any other ideas?"*

*"Sounds good to me, boss. And when I get hold of
that slimy reptile—"*

I was pleased by the klava, which I had with honey
and warmed cream. I forced myself not to think about
anything that mattered. I left a few extra coins on the
table to show them how much I appreciated their cup.
Loiosh preceded me out the door. He said everything
looked all right and I left the place, heading toward
Kelly's new headquarters. I avoided another contingent
of Phoenix Guards on the way. They really were all over
the place. None of the citizens seemed too happy with
them, and it seemed mutual.

The first thing I decided upon seeing Kelly's new
place was that it looked like Kelly's old place. The
brown was a different shade, and his flat was on the

right side instead of the left, and it was set a little farther back from the road, and there was just a little more space between buildings, but it had obviously been cast in the same mold.

I walked through the doorway. The flat itself had a real door. A heavy door, with a lock on it. I looked closer, just from curiosity. A *good* lock, and a *very* heavy door. It would take a great deal of work to break into this place, and it would be almost impossible to do silently. I wondered about windows and other doors. In any case, I decided I was impressed. Cawti had probably advised them. I started to clap, remembered, and, after a moment's hesitation, pounded on the door with my fist.

It was opened by my dear friend Gregory. His eyes widened as he saw me, but I didn't let him start in on me. I just pushed past him. It was rude, I know, and that still bothers me to this day, but I'll just have to learn to live with it.

One look told me that this flat was laid out the same as the other; I was almost certain I could walk into the next room and be in a library, through that to Kelly's office, and through that to a kitchen. But this room was cleaner; the cots were collapsed and pushed against the wall. The windows, I noticed, were heavily boarded.

Kelly was sitting in the room, talking to Natalia and a Teckla I didn't recognize. Cawti wasn't there. The talking stopped when I walked in, and they all stared at me. I smiled a big smile and said, "Is Cawti around?" Then they all looked at Kelly, except for Natalia, who kept looking at me. She said, "Not at the moment."

I said, "I'll wait, then," and watched them. Natalia kept watching me, the others watched Kelly, who squinted at me, his lips in a bit of a pout. Then, quite suddenly, he stood up and said, "Right. Come on back and I'll talk to you." He turned and headed toward the rear of the flat, assuming I would follow obediently. I cursed under my breath, smiling, and did so.

This office was as neat and well-organized as the other had been. I sat down on the other side of the desk.

Kelly folded his hands over his stomach and looked at me, his eyes performing their usual squint.

"So," he said. "You've decided to call in the Empire and force us to respond."

"Actually," I said, "I just came to see Cawti. Where is she?"

His expression didn't change, he just continued watching me. "You have a Plan," he said at last, pronouncing the capital letter, "and the rest of the world is filled with details that may or may not have something to do with it. You weren't out to get us, we're just a convenient tool."

He didn't put it as a question, which is partly why I felt stung; he was accusing me of something like what I had been thinking was wrong with him. I said, "My primary interest is actually saving Cawti's life."

"Not your own?" he shot back, his eyes squinting just a bit more.

"It's too late for that," I said. That startled him a little; he actually seemed surprised. I felt inordinately pleased about this. "So, as I said, I'd like to see Cawti. Will she be around later?"

He didn't answer. He just kept looking at me, his head back and his chin down, hands wrapped over his belly. I started to get mad. "Look," I told him, "you can play all the games you want to, just don't include me in them. I don't know what you're really after and I don't much care, all right? But, now or later, you're going to be carved up between the Empire and the Jhereg, and if I have any say in it my wife isn't going to be carved up with you. So you can drop the superior act; it doesn't impress me."

I was ready for him to blow up, but he didn't. His eyes hadn't even narrowed any more. He just kept watching me, as if he were studying me. He said, "You don't know what we're after? After all you've been through, you really don't know what we're after?"

I said, "I've heard the rhetoric."

"Have you listened to it?"

I snorted. "If what everybody around here parrots

originates with you, then I've heard what you have to say. That isn't what I came here for."

He leaned back a little more in his chair. "That's all you've heard, eh? The parroting of phrases?"

"Yeah. But as I said, that isn't—"

"Did you listen to the phrases being parroted?"

"I told you—"

"Have you never understood more than you could put into words? Many people only respond to the slogans—but they respond because the slogans are true and touch a spark in their hearts and their lives. And as for the ones who don't want to think for themselves, we teach them to anyway." Teach? I suddenly thought of what I'd overheard of them berating Cawti and wondered if that was what they called teaching. But Kelly continued, "Did you talk to Paresh? Or Natalia? Did you ever, once, *listen* to what they said?"

"Look—"

He shifted forward in his chair, just a bit. "But none of that matters. We aren't here to justify ourselves to you. We're Teckla and Easterners. In particular, we are that portion of that group that understands what it's doing."

"Yeah? What *are* you doing?"

"We are defending ourselves the only way we can, the only way there is—by uniting and using the power that we have due to our own role in society. With this, we can defend ourselves against the Empire, we can defend ourselves against the Jhereg, and we can defend ourselves against you."

La dee da. I said, "Can you?"

He said, "Yes."

"What's to stop me from killing you, say, now?"

He didn't bat an eyelash, which I call bravado, which a Dzur would consider brave and a Jhereg would consider stupid. He said, "Right. Go ahead, then."

"I could, you know."

"Then do it."

I cursed. I didn't kill him, of course. That was something I knew Cawti would never forgive me for, and it wouldn't accomplish anything anyway. I needed Kelly there to push his organization into the path of Herth and the Phoenix Guards so they could be neatly cleaned up. But I needed Cawti out of the way first.

I noticed that Kelly was still watching me. I said, "So, you exist only to defend yourselves, and the Easterners?"

"And the Teckla, yes. And the only defense is—but I forget; you aren't interested. You're so busy chasing fortune up over a mountain of corpses that you have no time to listen to anyone else, have you then?"

"Poetic, aren't you?" I said. "Have you ever read Torturi?"

"Yes," said Kelly. "I prefer Wint. Torturi is clever, but shallow."

"Um, yeah."

"Similar to Lartol."

"Yeah."

"They came out of the same school of poetry, and the same epoch, historically. It was after the reconstruction at the end of the ninth Vallista reign, and the aristocracy was feeling bitter toward—"

"All right, all right. You're quite well-read for a . . . whatever it is you are."

"I am a revolutionist."

"Yeah. Maybe you're a Vallista yourself. Creation and destruction, all wrapped up in one. Only you don't seem too effective at either."

"No," he said. "If I were of one of the Dragaeran Houses, it would be the Teckla."

I snorted. "You said it; I didn't."

"Yes. And it is another thing you don't understand."

"No doubt."

"But what I said is true for you as well—"

"Careful."

"And all human beings. The Teckla are known as a House of cowards. Is Paresh a coward?"

I licked my lips. "No."

"No. He has something worth fighting for. They are known as stupid and lazy as well. Does this match your experience?"

I started to say, "Yes," but then decided that, no, I couldn't say they were lazy. Stupid? Well, the Jhereg had been hoodwinking Teckla for years now, but that only meant we were clever. And, furthermore, there were so many of them it could be that I only ran across the stupid ones. It was hard to conceive of the total number of Teckla even within Adrilankha. Most of them were not customers of the Jhereg. "No," I said, "I guess not completely."

"The House of the Teckla," he said, "embodies all the traits of all the Dragaeran Houses. As does the Jhereg, by the way, and for much the same reason: Those Houses will allow others into their ranks with no questions asked. The aristocracy—the Dzur, the Dragons, the Lyorn, occasionally others—see this as a weakness. The Lyorn allow no one in; some of the others require the passing of a test. They think this strengthens their House, because it reinforces those things they desire—usually strength, quickness and cunning. These are thought to be the greatest virtues by the dominant culture—the culture of the aristocracy. If so, the mixing of blood without these traits must be a weakness. Because they think it's a weakness, you see it as a weakness, too. It is not; it is a strength.

"By requiring those traits, or whichever ones they do require, what are they leaving out that might occur on its own? All of these traits exist in some measure in the Teckla, the Jhereg and some Easterners—along with other things that we aren't even aware of, but that make us human. Think about what it means to be human. It's far more important than species or House." He stopped and studied me again.

I said, "I see. Well, now I've learned something about biology, history, and Teckla politics all in one sitting. That, and what is required to be a revolutionist. Thank you, it's been very instructive. Except I'm not interested in biology, I don't believe your history and I already knew what it takes to be a revolutionist. Right now I want to know what it takes to find Cawti."

He said, "Just what is it that you've found it takes to be a revolutionist?"

I knew he was trying to change the subject, but I couldn't resist. I said, "The worship of ideas to such an extent that you become totally ruthless toward people —friends, enemies and neutrals alike."

"The worship of ideas?" he said. "That's how you see it?"

"Yeah."

"And where do you suppose these ideas came from?"

"I can't see that it matters a whole lot."

"They come from people."

"Mostly dead people, I imagine."

He shook his head, slowly, but it seemed his eyes were twinkling, just a bit. "So," he said, "you have no ethics at all?"

"Don't bait me."

"Then you do?"

"Yeah."

"But you'll abandon them for anyone who matters to you?"

"I told you not to bait me. I won't tell you again."

"But what are professional ethics other than ideas that are more important than people?"

"Professional ethics guarantee that I always treat people as they ought to be treated."

"They guarantee that you do what's right, even if it isn't convenient at the moment?"

"Yes."

"Yes."

I said, "You're a smug bastard, aren't you?"

"No, but I can tell that you're speaking nonsense. You talk about our ideas as if they fell from the sky. They didn't. They grew out of our needs, out of our thoughts and out of our fight. Ideas aren't just thought up one day, and then people come along and decide to adopt them. Ideas are as much a product of their times as a particular summoning spell is the result of a particular Athyra reign. Ideas always express something real, even when they're wrong. People have been dying for ideas—sometimes incorrect ideas—since before history. Would that happen if those ideas weren't based on, and a product of, their lives and the world around them?

"As for us, no, we're not smug. Our strength is that we see ourselves as part of history, as part of society, instead of just individuals who happen to have the same problem. This means we can at least look for the right answers, even if we aren't completely right all the time. It certainly puts us a step ahead of the individualists. It's all well and good to recognize that you have a problem and try to solve it, but for the Easterners and Teckla in this world, these aren't problems that an individual can solve."

I guess when you get in the habit of making speeches it's hard to stop. When he'd run down, I said, "I'm an individual. I solved them. I got out of there and made something of myself."

"How many bodies did you climb over to do it?"

"Forty-three."

"Well?"

"What of it?"

"What of it yourself?"

I stared at him. He was squinting hard again. Some of the things he was saying were uncomfortably close to things I'd been thinking about myself; but I didn't go around building elaborate political positions around my insecurities, nor inciting rebellion as if I knew better than the rest of the world how everything ought to be.

I said, "If I'm so worthless, why are you wasting your time talking to me?"

"Because Cawti is valuable to us. She's still new, but she could turn into an excellent revolutionist. She's having trouble with you, and it's hurting her work. I want it settled."

I controlled myself with an effort. "That fits," I said. "Okay, then, I'll even let you manipulate me into helping you manipulate Cawti so she can help you manipulate the entire population of South Adrilankha. That's how it works, isn't it? All right, I'll go along. Tell me where she is."

"No, that isn't how it works. I'm not making any deals with you. You called in the Phoenix Guards to manipulate us into an adventure that would destroy us. Whatever reasons you had for this, it didn't work. We aren't getting involved in any adventures now. We held a mass meeting yesterday at which we urged everyone to stay calm and not to allow the Guards to provoke an incident. We're ready to defend ourselves against any attacks, but we won't allow ourselves to be endangered by—"

"Oh, stop it. You're doomed anyway. Do you really think you can stand up to Herth? He has more hired killers working for him than Verra has hairs on her . . . head. If I hadn't forced him into action, he would have destroyed you as soon as he realized you weren't going to back down."

Kelly asked, "Does he have more hired killers than there are Easterners and Teckla in Adrilankha?"

"Heh. I don't know of *any* professionals who are Teckla, and I'm just about the only Easterner I know."

"Professional killers? No. But professional revolutionists, yes. This Jhereg killed Franz, and we mobilized half of South Adrilankha. He killed Sheryl and we mobilized the other half. You've brought the Phoenix Guards in, probably thinking you were working on some big plan to solve all your problems, when in fact you did exactly what the Empire required of you—you gave them a pretext to move in. All right, here they are, and they can't do anything. The instant they overstep themselves, we'll take the whole city."

"If you're that close, why don't you do it?"

"We don't want it yet. The time isn't right for it. Oh, we could hold the city for a while, but the rest of the country isn't ready, and we can't stand against the rest of the country. But if we have to, we will, because it will serve as an example and we'll grow because of it. The Empire can't crush us because the rest of the country would rise; they see us as representing them."

"So they're just going to give you what you want?"

He shook his head. "They can't fully investigate the murders because it would expose how closely the Jhereg is tied to the Empire, and the Jhereg itself would have to fight back and total chaos would ensue. They know what we *can* do, but they don't know what we're *going* to do, so all they can do is move their troops in, and hope that we make a mistake and lose the confidence of the masses so they can crush us—our movement and the citizens alike."

I stared at him. "Do you really believe all that? You still haven't told me what's going to stop Herth from bringing six or seven assassins in here and just cleaning you out."

"Weren't you, yourself, trying to play Herth off against the Empire?"

"Yeah."

"Well, you didn't have to. We almost took the city the last time the Jhereg killed one of our people, and the Jhereg know very well that if it happens again the Empire will have to move against them. How is that going to affect this Herth fellow?"

"Hard to say. He's getting desperate."

Kelly shook his head again and leaned back in his chair. I studied him. Who did he remind me of? Aliera, perhaps, with that cocksure attitude. Maybe Morrolan, with his feeling that, well, of course he could destroy anyone who got in his way, because that's just how things are. I don't know. There was no question that the man was brilliant, but—I didn't know then, and I still don't.

I was trying to figure out my next riposte when Kelly's head shot up, and at the same time Loiosh spun around. Kelly said, "Hello, Cawti."

I didn't turn. Loiosh started hissing and I heard Rocza hiss back. Loiosh flew off and I heard wings flapping and much hissing. Cawti said, "Hello, Vlad. Do those two remind you of anything?"

I did turn around then, and there were circles under

her eyes. She looked haggard and worn. I wanted to hold her and tell her it was all right, except I didn't dare, and it wasn't. Kelly stood up and left. I suppose he expected me to be grateful.

When he was gone, I said, "Cawti, I want you out of this. This little group is going to be crushed and I want you somewhere safe."

She said, "Yeah, I figured that out last night, after I left."

Her voice was quiet as she spoke, and I heard no harshness or hate in it. I said, "Does it change anything?"

"I'm not sure. You're asking me to choose between my beliefs and my love."

I swallowed. "Yeah, I guess that's what I'm doing."

"Are you sure you have to?"

"I have to make sure you're safe."

"What about you?"

"That's another question. It doesn't apply to this."

"The only reason you did all that was—"

"To save your life, dammit!"

"Stop it, Vlad. Please."

"Sorry."

"You did it because you're so full of how powerful Herth is that you can't see how weak he is compared to the armed might of the masses."

I started to tell her to stop that noise about the "armed might of the masses," but I didn't. I thought about it for a minute. Well, yeah, if the masses were armed, and had leaders they trusted and all that, yeah, they could be powerful. If, if, if. I said, "What if you're wrong?"

She actually stopped and thought about that for a moment, which surprised me. Then she said, "Remember outside the old place, when the Phoenix Guards showed up? Herth just stood there while that Dragonlord cut his face. Herth hated her and wanted to kill her, but he just stood there and took it. Who was more powerful?"

"Okay, the Dragonlord. Go on."

"The Dragonlord just stood there, troops and all, while Kelly laid down our demands. Can you really think that Kelly is more powerful than a Dragon warrior?"

"No."

"Neither can I. The power was the armed might of the masses. You *saw* it. You think you, by yourself, are stronger than it is?"

"I don't know."

"You admit you might be wrong?"

I sighed. "Yeah."

"Then why don't you stop trying to protect me? It's insulting, in addition to everything else."

I said, "I *can't*, Cawti. Don't you see that? I just can't. You don't have the right to throw your life away. No one does."

"Are you sure I'm throwing my life away?"

I closed my eyes, and felt the start of tears that I hadn't been able to shed the night before. I stopped them. I said, "Let me think about it, all right?"

"All right."

"Are you coming back home?"

"Let's wait until this is over, then we'll see where we are."

"Over? When will it be over?"

"When the Empress withdraws her troops."

"Oh."

Loiosh came back in and landed on my shoulder. I said, *"Everything settled, chum?"*

"Pretty much, boss. I'm not going to be flying too well for a few days. She got in a good one on my right wing."

"I see."

"Nothing to worry about."

"Yeah."

I stood up and walked past Cawti without touching her. Kelly was in the other room, deep in conversation with Gregory and a few others. None of them looked up as I left. I stepped outside, carefully, but saw no one suspicious. I teleported back home, deciding that

Kragar could handle things at the office better than I could right now.

The stairs up to my flat seemed long and steep, and my legs felt leaden. Once inside, I collapsed on the couch again and stared off into space for a while. I thought about cleaning the place up, but it didn't really need it and I didn't have the energy.

Loiosh asked if I'd like to see a show and I didn't.

I spent a couple of hours sharpening my rapier because it seemed likely I'd be needing it soon. Then I stared off into space for a while, but no ideas fell from the sky and landed on me.

After a while I got up and selected a book of poems by Wint. I opened the book at random, and was at a poem called "Smothered."

> ". . . Was it for naught I bled for thee,
> Defying omnipotent powers?
>
> The blood was mine; the battle, thine,
> To smother in bright-blooming flowers. . . ."

I read it to the end, and wondered. Maybe I was wrong. It didn't seem obscure at all, just then.

16-

. . .& repair cut in left side.

I woke up in the chair, the book on my lap. I felt stiff
and uncomfortable, which is natural after sleeping in
a chair. I stretched out to loosen my muscles, then
bathed. It was pretty early. I put some wood in the stove
and kicked it up with sorcery, then cooked a few eggs
and warmed up some herb bread that Cawti had made
before she left. It was especially good with garlic butter.
The klava helped, and it helped to do the dishes and
clean up the place. By the time that was done I felt almost ready for the day.

I wrote a few letters of instruction to various people,
in case of my demise. I kept them terse. I sat down and
thought for a while. I hate, I mean *hate*, changing a plan
at the last minute, but there was no way around it.
Cawti wasn't going to be safe. Furthermore, there was
the chance that Kelly was right. No, there just wasn't
any way to arrange for all of my enemies to neatly destroy each other; I had to do something else. I ran down
the events of the past few days and my options for dealing with the situation I had created, and eventually hit
on the idea of bringing my grandfather into things.

Yeah, that might work, as long as he didn't show up
while there was still fighting going on. I put what passed

for the finishing touches on the idea.

I concentrated on Kragar, and soon he said, *"Who is it?"*

"It's me."

"What is it?"

"Can you reach Ishtvan?"

"Yeah."

"Give him Kelly's new address in South Adrilankha, and have him wait there, out of sight, this afternoon."

"Okay. Anything else?"

"Yeah." I gave him the rest of his instructions.

"Do you really think he'll go for it, Vlad?"

"I don't know. Right now it's our best shot, though."

"Okay."

Then I drew my rapier and made a few passes in the air, loosening up my wrist. Supple but firm, my grandfather always said.

I checked all of my weapons as carefully as I ever have, then I organized my thoughts and teleported. Unless I was very much mistaken, today would be it.

There was a nasty wind whipping through the streets of South Adrilankha. It wasn't terribly chilly, but it had something of a sting from the dust it kicked up. It played havoc with my cloak as I leaned against a wall near Kelly's headquarters. I moved to a place out of the wind that also provided better concealment, although not quite as good a view. I watched the Phoenix Guards march by in neat groups of four. They were trying to maintain order where there was no disorder, and some of them, mostly the Dragons, were either bored or grumbling. The Teckla seemed to be enjoying it; they could strut around the street and be important. They were the ones who were constantly gripping the hilts of their weapons.

The interesting thing was how easy it was to tell the political affiliations of the passers-by. There were no headbands, but they weren't necessary. Some people would walk the streets furtively, or go quickly to their destinations as if they were afraid of being out on the streets. Others seemed to savor the tension in the air; they would walk with their heads up, glancing about themselves as if something might *happen* at any moment, and they didn't want to miss it.

By early afternoon Ishtvan was probably around somewhere, though I didn't see him. Quaysh was, too, I assumed. Quaysh knew that I knew he was there, but I felt hopeful that Quaysh didn't know Ishtvan was there.

I reached Kragar again. *"Anything exciting happen?"*

"No. Ishtvan is there."

"Good. So am I. All right, send the message."

"You're sure?"

"Yeah. Now or never. I won't have the nerve again."

"Okay. And the sorceress?"

"Yes. Send her to the apothecary across from Kelly's. And have her wait. Does she know me by sight?"

"I doubt it. But you're pretty easy to describe. I'll make sure she recognizes you."

"Okay. Have at it."

"Right, Vlad."

And we were committed.

The note that Herth would be receiving was quite simple. It said: "I'm prepared to compromise, if you'll arrange for the removal of the Phoenix Guards. Because of the Guards, I can't leave my flat. You may arrive at your convenience. —Kelly."

Its strength was its weakness: It was too obvious to be the fake that it was. But Kelly and Herth couldn't know each other well enough to communicate psionically, so messages were required. Herth was bound to have a very low opinion of Kelly, which was also important. In order for this to work, Herth had to believe that Kelly was scared of the Phoenix Guards, and Herth had to think that Kelly was ignorant of how much of a threat these guards were to a Jhereg. *I* knew that Kelly was really aware of all that, but presumably Herth didn't.

So, the questions were: Would Herth show up in person? How many bodyguards would he bring? And, what other precautions would he take?

The sorceress arrived before anything else happened. I didn't recognize her. She was a tall Jhereg with black hair in tight curls. Her mouth was harsh and she showed some signs of Athyra in her ancestry. She wore the Jhereg grey. She entered the shop. I followed carefully. She saw me as I entered and said, "Lord Taltos?" I nodded. She gestured at Kelly's building. "You want a block to prevent anyone from teleporting out. Is that all?"

"Yes."

"When?"

I pulled out a coin, studied it with eye and fingers for a moment, and handed it to her. "When this heats up."

"All right," she said.

I left the shop, still being very careful. I didn't want to be attacked just yet. I resumed my old position and waited. A few minutes later a Dragaeran in the colors of House Jhereg showed up.

I said, *"All right, Loiosh. Take off."*

"Are you sure?"

"Yeah."

"Okay, boss. Good luck."

He flew away. That put a time limit on things. The bloody part of the day had to be over within, I guessed, about thirty minutes. I drew a dagger and held it low, and pushed myself deeper into the shadows cast by the tall old house I was standing against. Then I put the dagger away and fingered my rapier, but didn't draw it. I touched Spellbreaker, but left it wrapped around my wrist. I squeezed my hands into and out of fists.

What was going on inside Kelly's flat, I could only guess at. But I had no doubt that the Jhereg had been a messenger from Herth. He would have walked in and said, "Herth is on his way." Neither Kelly nor the messenger would know why, so—

Natalia and Paresh left the building, walking in opposite directions.

—Kelly would send for help. From whom? From the

"people," of course. My earlier plan had required this, and I could have then informed the Phoenix Guards of it and incited mutual destruction. I wasn't going to do that now, however, because Cawti was still part of it.

Four Jhereg showed up. Enforcers, hired muscle, legmen. Two of them went inside to check the place over, while the others studied the area, looking for people like me. I stayed hidden. If Ishtvan was there, he did too. Likewise Quaysh. I was getting a lesson in how easy it is to hide on a city street, and how hard it is to find someone who is hiding.

About seven minutes later Herth showed up, along with Bajinok and another three bodyguards. They entered the flat. I concentrated for a moment and performed a very simple spell. A coin heated up. A teleport block occurred around Kelly's flat.

Just about that time, Easterners and an occasional Teckla began to congregate on the street. One of the legmen outside went in, presumably to report on this development. He came out again. Then Phoenix Guards began to collect on the opposite side of the street. In a surprisingly short time—like five minutes, maybe—there was a repeat of the scene before: about two hundred armed Easterners on one side, eighty or so Phoenix Guards on the other. That to you, Kelly. Instant confrontation, courtesy of Baronet Taltos.

Trouble was, I no longer wanted a confrontation. That plan had involved having Cawti out of the way, so I could kill Herth while Ishtvan killed Quaysh and the Guards killed Kelly and his band. But I hadn't sent the messages informing the Phoenix Guards of this occurrence; they had found out on their own. Damn them anyway.

Well, there was no way of pulling out at this stage. By now Herth would be inside, he would have realized that the message didn't come from Kelly, and he would have realized that there was a teleport block around the building. He would deduce that I was out here somewhere, waiting to kill him. What would he do? Well, he might just try to come out, hoping that I wouldn't try

anything with the Phoenix Guards all around. Or he
might call for more bodyguards, surround himself completely and walk out of the place; far enough away to be
able to teleport. He was probably pretty unhappy now.

The lieutenant who'd been there last time was not in
sight. Instead, the commander of the Phoenix Guard
was an old Dragaeran who wore the blue and white of
the House of the Tiassa beneath the gold cloak of the
Phoenix. He had that peculiar, stiff-yet-relaxed pose of
the longtime soldier. Had he been an Easterner, he
would have had a long mustache to pull. As it was, he
scratched the side of his nose from time to time. Other
than that, he hardly moved. I noticed that his blade was
very long but lightweight, and I decided that I didn't
want to fight him. Then it occurred to me that this was
an old Tiassa in command of Phoenix Guards, and I realized that it was probably the Lord Khaavren himself,
the Brigadier of the Guards. I was impressed.

Easterners and Guards continued to gather, and now
Kelly stepped outside and looked around, along with
Natalia and a couple of others. Soon they went back in.
I was able to tell nothing from watching Kelly. A bit
later Gregory and Paresh went out and began speaking
to the Easterners, quietly. I assumed they were telling
them to remain calm.

I flexed my fingers. I closed my eyes and concentrated
on the building across the street. I remembered the
hallway. I saw the broken porcelain below next to my
right foot, but ignored it; it could have been cleaned up.
I called up a picture of the reddish stain that was probably liquor on the floor and against the wall. Then I
remembered the stairs in the middle of the hall, probably leading down to a cellar, with a curtain at the top.
The ceiling above it was pitted with broken paint and
chipped woodwork. A frayed rope dangled from it. The
rope had probably once held a candelabrum. I remembered the thickness of the rope and the way the frayed
end had hung and the shape of the frays. I recalled the
layer of dust just inside the curtain. And the curtain
itself, woven in zigzags of dark brown and an ugly, dirty

blue, both against a background that might once have been green. The smell of the hallway, compressed, dust-choked and stuffy, so thick I could almost taste it; I *could* taste the dust in my mouth.

I decided I had it. I held it there, fixed, and called upon my link to the Orb, and the power rushed through me to the forms I created and shaped and spun, until they matched, in a deep yet inexplicable way, the picture and scent and taste I held in my mind.

I drew them in, my eyes tightly closed, and I knew I had caught *somewhere*, because the sickening movement began in my bowels. I gave the last twist and opened my eyes, and, yes, I was there. It didn't look or smell quite the way I remembered it, but close enough. In any case, it hid me quite effectively.

I was assuming that there were bodyguards in the hallway, so I tried to keep silent. Have you ever felt you were about to throw up, and yet had to keep silent? But let's not dwell on that; I managed. After a while I risked a look past the curtain. I saw a bodyguard standing in the hall. He was about as alert as it is possible to be when nothing is immediately happening, which isn't all that alert. I ducked my head back without being seen. I looked the other way, toward the back door, but didn't see anyone. There may have been one or two outside the back door, or just inside the back entrance to the flat itself, but I could ignore them for now either way.

I listened closely and I could make out Herth's voice, speaking peremptorily. So he was inside. He was well-protected, of course. My options seemed rather limited. I could try to pick off his protection one by one. That is, find a way to quiet these two without alerting those inside, remove the bodies and wait until someone investigated, repeating as needed. It was attractive in a way, but I had real doubts about my ability to handle that many without a noise; and, in any case, Herth might duck out at any moment if he decided that was his best chance.

On the other hand, there was only one other option,

and that was stupid. I mean, *really* stupid. The only time for doing something that stupid is when you're so mad you can't think clearly, you expect to die anyway, you have weeks of frustration built up to the point where you want to explode and you figure maybe you can take a few of them with you, and, generally, you just don't care any more.

I decided this was the perfect time.

I checked all my weapons, then drew two thin and extremely sharp throwing knives. I kept my arms at my sides so the knives, if not hidden, at least wouldn't be obvious. I stepped out into the hall.

He saw me at once, and stared. I was walking toward him, and I seem to recall that I had a smile on my lips. Yes, in fact I'm sure of it. Maybe that's what stopped him, but he just stared at me. My pulse was racing by then. I kept walking, waiting until either I was close enough or he moved. My guess, looking back on those ten steps down the hall, was that I would have been cut down at once if I'd tried to rush him, but by walking toward him, smiling, I threw him out of his reckoning. He stared at me as if hypnotized, making no motion until I was right up to him.

Then I nailed him, one knife in his stomach, which is one of the most disabling of non-fatal wounds. He crumbled to the floor right at my feet.

I took a knife from my boot; one I could throw as well as cut or stab with. I entered the room.

Two bodyguards were just looking up toward the doorway and tentatively reaching for weapons. The messenger was sitting on a couch with his eyes closed, looking bored. Bajinok stood next to Herth, who was talking to Kelly. I could see Kelly's face, but not Herth's. Kelly wasn't pleased. Cawti stood next to Kelly and she spotted me at once. Paresh and Gregory were in the room, along with three Easterners and a Teckla who I didn't recognize.

Also next to Herth was a bodyguard who was staring right at me. Whose eyes were widening. Who had a knife in his hand. Who was ready to throw it at me. Who fell with my knife high on the right side of his chest.

As he fell, he managed to release his weapon, but I slipped to the side and it only grazed my waist. As I avoided it, I turned to kill Herth, but Bajinok had stepped in front of him. I cursed to myself and moved farther into the room, looking for my next set of enemies.

The other two bodyguards drew weapons, but I was faster than I thought I'd be. I sent each of them a small dart coated with a poison that would make their muscles constrict, and I put a couple of other things into their bodies as well. They went down, got up, and went down again.

Meanwhile, my rapier was out and I had a dagger in my left hand. Bajinok pulled a lepip from somewhere, which was nasty because it could break my blade if it hit. Herth was staring at me over Bajinok's shoulder; he hadn't yet drawn a weapon. I don't know, maybe he didn't have one. I avoided a strike from Bajinok and riposted—taking him cleanly through the chest. He gave one spasm and fell. I looked over at the guy who'd acted as a messenger. He had a dagger in his hand and was half standing up. He dropped the dagger and sat down again, his hands well clear of his body.

It had been less than ten seconds since I'd stepped into the room. Now three bodyguards were down in various stages of discomfort and uselessness (not to mention two more in the hall), Bajinok was probably dying, and the remaining Jhereg on Herth's side had declared himself out of the action.

I couldn't believe it had worked.

Neither could Herth.

He said, "What are you, anyway?"

I sheathed my rapier and drew my belt dagger. I didn't answer him because I don't talk to my targets; it puts the relationship on entirely the wrong basis. I heard something behind me and saw Cawti's eyes widen. I threw myself to the side of the room, rolled, and came to a kneeling position.

A body—one that I hadn't put there—was lying on the floor. I noticed that Cawti had a dagger out, held down to her side. Herth still hadn't moved. I checked the body to make sure it wasn't anything more than that. It wasn't. It was Quaysh. There was a short iron spike protruding from his back. Thank you, Ishtvan, wherever you are.

I stood up again and turned to the messenger. "Get out," I said. "If those two bodyguards outside start to come in here, my people outside will kill you." He might well have wondered why, if I had people outside, they hadn't killed the bodyguards. But he didn't say anything; he just left.

I took a step toward Herth and raised my dagger. At this point I didn't care who saw me, or if I was going to be turned over to the Empire. I wanted this finished.

Kelly said, "Wait."

I stopped, mostly from sheer disbelief. I said, "What?"

"Don't kill him."

"Are you nuts?" I took another step. Herth had absolutely no expression on his face.

"I mean it," said Kelly.

"I'm glad."

"Don't kill him."

I stopped and stepped back a pace. "Okay," I said. "Why?"

"He's *our* enemy. We've been fighting him for years. We don't need you to step in and settle it for us, and we don't need an Imperial, or even a Jhereg, investigation into his death."

I said, "This may be hard for you to believe, but I don't really give a teckla's squeal what you want. If I don't kill him now, I'm dead. I thought I was anyway, but things seem to have worked out so that I might live. I'm not going to—"

"I think you can arrange for him not to come after

you, without killing him yourself."

I blinked. Finally I said, "All right, how?"

"I don't know," said Kelly. "But look at his situation: You've battered his organization almost out of existence. It's going to take everything he has just to put it together. He is in a position of weakness. You can manage something."

I looked at Herth. He still showed no expression. I said, "At best, that just means he's going to wait."

Kelly said, "Maybe."

I turned back to Kelly. "How do you know so much about how we operate and what kind of situation he's in?"

"It's our business to know everything that affects us and those we represent. We've been fighting him for years, one way or another. We have to know him and how he operates."

"Okay. Maybe. But you still haven't told me why I should let him live."

Kelly squinted at me. "Do you know," he said, "that you are a walking contradiction? Your background is from South Adrilankha, you are an Easterner, yet you have been working all your life to deny this, to adopt the attitudes of the Dragaerans, to almost *be* a Dragaeran, and more, an aristocrat—"

"That's a lot of—"

"At times, you affect the speech patterns of the aristocracy. You are working to become, not rich, but *powerful*, because that is what the aristocracy values above all things. And yet, at the same time, you wear a mustache to assert your Eastern origins, and you identify with Easterners so much that, I'm told, you have never plied your trade on one, and, in fact, turned down an offer to murder Franz."

"So, what does this—?"

"Now you have to choose. I'm not asking you to give up your profession, despicable as it is. I'm not asking you for *anything*, in fact. I'm telling you that it is in the interest of our people that you not murder this person. Do what you want." He turned away.

I chewed on my lip, amazed at first that I was even thinking about it. I shook my head. I thought about Franz, who was actually pleased to have his name used for propaganda after he died, and Sheryl, who would probably have felt the same, and I thought about all that Kelly had said to me over the last few times we spoke, and about Natalia, and I remembered the talk with Paresh, so long ago it seemed, and the look he'd given me at the end. Now I understood it.

Most people never have the chance to choose what side they're on, but I did. That's what Paresh was telling me, and Sheryl and Natalia. Franz had thought I had chosen. Cawti and I had reached a point where we could choose our sides. Cawti had chosen, and now I had to. I wondered if I could choose to stay in the middle.

It suddenly didn't matter that I was standing in a crowd of strangers. I turned to Cawti and said, "I should join you. I know that. But I can't. Or I won't. I guess that's what it comes down to." She didn't say anything. Neither did anyone else. In the awful silence of that ugly little room, I just kept talking.

"Whatever this thing is that I've become is incapable of looking beyond itself. Yes, I'd like to do something for the greater good of humanity, if you want to call it that. But I can't, and we're both stuck with that. I can cry and wail as much as I want and it doesn't change what I am or what you are or anything else."

Still, no one said anything. I turned to Kelly and said, "You will probably never know how much I hate you. I respect you, and I respect what you're doing, but you've diminished me in my own eyes, and in Cawti's. I can't forgive you for that."

For just an instant then he was human. "Have I done that? We're doing what we have to do. Every decision we make is based on what is necessary. Is it really I who has done this to you?"

I shrugged and turned toward Herth. Might as well make it complete. "I hate you most of all," I said. "Much more than I hate him. I mean, this goes beyond business. I want to kill you, Herth. And I'd love to do it slow; torture you the way you tortured me. That's what I want."

He was still showing no expression, damn his eyes. I wanted to see him cringe, at least, but he wouldn't. Maybe it would have been better for him if he had. Maybe not, too. But staring at him, I almost lost it again. I was holding a stiletto, my favorite kind of weapon for a simple assassination; I longed to make him feel it, and having him just stare at me like that was too much. I just couldn't take it. I grabbed him by the throat and flung him against a wall, held the point of my blade against his left eye. I said some things to him that I don't remember but were never above the level of curses. Then I said, "They want me to let you live. Okay, bastard, you can live. For a while. But I'm watching you, all right? You send anyone after me and you've had it. Got that?"

He said, "I won't send anyone after you."

I shook my head. I didn't believe him, but I figured I'd at least bought some time. I said to Cawti, "I'm going home. Coming with me?"

She looked at me, her forehead creased and sorrow in her eyes. I turned away.

As Herth started to move toward the door, I heard the sound of steel on steel from behind me, and a heavy sword came flying into the room. Then a Jhereg came in, backing up. At his throat was a rapier, and attached to the rapier was my grandfather. Ambrus was on his shoulder. Loiosh flew into the room.

"Noish-pa!"

"Yes, Vladimir. You wished to see me?"

"Sort of," I said. I had some mad in me that hadn't washed away yet, but it was going. I decided I had to get outside of there before I exploded.

Kelly said, "Hello, Taltos," to my grandfather.

They exchanged nods.

"Wait here," I said to no one in particular. I walked out into the hall, and the bodyguard I had wounded was still moaning and holding his stomach, although he had removed the knife. There was another one next to him who was holding his right leg. I could see wounds on both legs and both arms and a shoulder. They were small wounds, but probably deep. I was pleased that my grandfather was still as good as I remembered. I walked past them carefully and out into the street. There was now a solid line of armed Easterners and an equally solid line of Phoenix Guards. There were no Jhereg bodyguards there anymore, however.

I walked through the Guards until I found their commander. "Lord Khaavren?" I said.

He looked at me and his face tightened. He nodded once.

I said, "There will be no trouble. It was a mistake. These Easterners are going to leave now. I just want to tell you that."

He stared at me for a moment, then looked away as if I were so much carrion. I turned and went into the apothecary. I found the sorceress and said, "Okay, you can lift it. And if you want to earn some more, Herth will be coming out onto the street soon, and I think he'd appreciate a teleport back home."

"Thanks," she said. "It's been a pleasure."

I nodded and walked back toward Kelly's flat. As I did so, Herth emerged with several wounded bodyguards, including one who had to be helped along. Herth didn't even look at me. I went past him, and I saw the sorceress approach and speak to him.

When I went back inside, my grandfather was nowhere to be seen and neither was Cawti. Loiosh said, *"They've gone back into Kelly's study."*

"Good."

"Why did you send me instead of reaching him psionically?"

"My grandfather doesn't approve of it, except for emergencies."

"Wasn't this an emergency?"

"Yeah. Well, I also wanted you out of the way so I could go ahead and do something stupid."

"I see. Well, did you?"

"Yeah. I even got away with it."

"*Oh. Does that mean everything's all right now?*"

I looked back toward the study where my grandfather was talking with Cawti. "*Probably not,*" I said. "*But it's out of my hands. I thought I'd probably be dead after this, and I wanted someone here who could take care of Cawti.*"

"*But what about Herth?*"

"*He promised to leave me alone in front of witnesses. That will keep him honest for a few weeks, anyway.*"

"*And after that?*"

"*We'll just have to see.*"

17 –

1 Pocket Handkerchief: clean & press

The next day I received word that the troops had been withdrawn from South Adrilankha. Cawti didn't show up. But I hadn't really expected her to.

To take my mind off things, I took a walk around my neighborhood. I was beginning to enjoy the feeling that I was in no more danger than I'd been before this nonsense started. It might not last, but I'd enjoy it while I could. I even walked a bit outside of my area, just because walking felt so good. I hit a couple of inns that I don't usually visit and that was fine. I was careful not to get drunk, even though it probably wouldn't have mattered.

I passed by the oracle I'd been to so long before and thought about going in, but I didn't. It did make me wonder, though, what I ought to do with all of that money. It was clear that I wasn't going to be building Cawti a castle. Even if she came back to me, I doubted she'd want one. And the idea of buying a higher title in the Jhereg seemed ludicrous. That left—

Which is when the solution hit me.

My first reaction was to laugh, but I couldn't afford to laugh at any idea just then, and besides, I'd look foolish standing in the middle of the street laughing.

The more I thought about it, though, the more sense it made. From Herth's perspective, that is. I mean, as Kelly had said, the man was almost washed up; this let him get out alive and removed any need on his part to kill me.

From my end it was even easier than that. It would entail many administrative problems, of course, but I could use a few administrative problems. Hmmm. I finished the walk without incident.

Two days later I was sitting in my office, taking care of the details of getting things operating again and a few other matters. Melestav came in.

"Yeah?"

"A messenger just arrived from Herth, boss."

"Oh, yeah? What did he have to say?"

"He said, 'Yes.' He said you'd know what it was about. He's waiting for a reply."

"Well I'll be damned," I said. "Yeah. I know what it's about."

"Any instructions?"

"Yeah. Go into the treasury and pull out fifty thousand Imperials."

"Fifty *thousand*?"

"That's right."

"But—all right. Then what?"

"Give it to the messenger. Arrange for an escort. Make sure it gets to Herth."

"All right, boss. Whatever you say."

"Then come back in here; we have a lot of work to do. And send Kragar in."

"Okay."

"I'm already here."

"Huh? Oh."

"What just happened?"

"What we wanted to. We have the prostitution, which we'll have to close down or clean up, the strong-arm stuff, which we'll kill, and the gambling, cleaners, and small stuff, which we can leave alone."

"You mean it worked?"

"Yeah. We just bought South Adrilankha."

I got home late that night and found Cawti asleep on the couch. I looked down at her. Her dark, dark hair was in disarray over her thin, proud face. Her cheekbones stood out in the light of the single lamp, and her fine brows were drawn together as she slept, as if she was puzzled by something a dream was telling her.

She was still beautiful, inside and out. It hurt to look at her. I shook her gently. She opened her eyes, smiled wanly and sat up.

"Hello, Vlad."

I sat down next to her, but not too close. "Hello," I said.

She blinked sleep out of her eyes. After a moment she said, "I had a long talk with Noish-pa. I guess that was what you wanted, wasn't it?"

"I knew I couldn't talk to you. I hoped he could find the way to say things I couldn't."

She nodded.

I said, "Do you want to tell me about it?"

"I'm not sure. What I said to you, a long time ago now, about how unhappy you are and why, that's all true, I think."

"Yeah."

"And I think what I'm doing, working with Kelly, is right, and I'm going to keep doing it."

"Yeah."

"But it isn't the whole answer to every question, either. Once I decided that I'd do this, I thought it would solve everything, and I treated you unfairly. I'm sorry. The rest of life doesn't stop because of my activities. I'm working with Kelly because that's my duty, but it doesn't end there. I also have a duty toward you."

I looked down. When she didn't go on, I said, "I don't want you coming back to me because you feel it's your duty."

She sighed. "I see what you mean. No, that isn't how I meant it. The problem is that you were right, I *should* have spoken to you about it. But I couldn't bring myself to risk—to risk what we have. Do you see what I mean?"

I stared at her. Do you know, that had never occurred to me? I mean, I knew I felt frightened and insecure; but I never thought that *she* could feel that way, too. I said, "I love you."

She made a gesture with her arm and I moved over to her and put my arm around and held her. After a while I said, "Are you moving back in?"

She said, "Should I? We still have a lot to work out."

I thought about my latest purchase and chuckled. "You don't know the half of it."

She said, "Hmm?"

I said, "I've just bought South Adrilankha."

She stared. "You *bought* South Adrilankha? From Herth?"

"Yeah."

She shook her head. "Yes, I guess we do have things to talk about."

"Cawti, it saved my life. Doesn't that—?"

"Not now."

I didn't say anything. A moment later she said, "I'm committed now; to Kelly, to the Easterners, to the Teckla. I still don't know how you feel about that."

"Neither do I," I said. "I don't know if it would be easier or harder to work it out with you living here again. All I know is that I miss you, that it hurts to go to sleep without you."

She nodded. Then she said, "I'll come back then, if you want me to, and we'll try to work it out."

I said, "I want you to."

We didn't celebrate then, or anything, but we held each other, and for me that was a celebration, and the tears I shed onto her shoulder felt as clean and good as the laugh of a condemned man, unexpectedly freed.

Which, in a way, described me quite well, just then.

Stories
✠✠ of ✠✠
Swords and Sorcery

⚜⚜⚜⚜⚜⚜⚜⚜⚜⚜⚜⚜⚜⚜⚜⚜⚜⚜⚜

☐ 76600-5	**SILVERGLASS** J.F. Rivkin	$2.95
☐ 38553-2	**JHEREG**, Steven Brust	$2.95
☐ 11452-0	**CONAN**, Robert E. Howard	$2.95
☐ 81653-3	**TOMOE GOZEN** Jessica Amanda Salmonson	$2.75
☐ 13897-7	**DAUGHTER OF WITCHES** Patricia C. Wrede	$2.95
☐ 10264-6	**CHANGELING**, Roger Zelazny	$2.95
☐ 79197-2	**SWORDS AND DEVILTRY** Fritz Leiber	$2.75
☐ 81466-2	**TO DEMONS BOUND** **(Swords of Raemllyn #1)** Robert E. Vardeman and Geo. W. Proctor	$2.95
☐ 04913-3	**BARD**, Keith Taylor	$2.95
☐ 89644-8	**WITCH BLOOD**, Will Shetterly	$2.95

♣♣♣♣♣♣♣♣♣♣♣♣♣♣♣♣♣♣♣

BESTSELLING
Science Fiction
and
Fantasy